Note To Readers

In The American Adventure Book One, *The Mayflower Adventure*, twelve-year-old John Smythe and his ten-year-old sister, Sarah, sail to America, the New World, on the *Mayflower* with their parents, friends, and the London Strangers.

Mischievous John and quiet, freckle-faced Sarah are fictional characters who represent real children and teens who came to America from England and Holland. The hardships they faced in their escape to freedom, both on board ship and trying to survive in a new land, helped make our country a place where all can worship God in whatever way they choose.

Plymouth Pioneers is filled with real incidents and real people: Governor William Bradford, Captain Myles Standish, Mary Allerton, and many others. If it had not been for the friendly Indians Samoset, Squanto, and Chief Massasoit, all those who came on the *Mayflower* would have died of starvation during the first long and tragic year in Plymouth Colony.

PLYMOUTH PIONEERS

Colleen L. Reece

BARBOUR
PUBLISHING, INC.
Uhrichsville, Ohio

© MCMXCVII by Barbour Publishing, Inc.

ISBN 1-57748-060-0

Published by Barbour Publishing, Inc., P.O. Box 719, Uhrichsville, Ohio 44683
http://www.barbourbooks.com

 Member of the
Evangelical Christian
Publishers Association

Printed in the United States of America.

Cover illustration by Chris Cocozza.
Inside illustrations by Adam Wallenta.

CHAPTER 1

A Swift Runner

"Captain Standish!" Twelve-year-old John Smythe raced down the deck of the *Mayflower*. Panting as much from excitement as running, he stopped before the red-faced, mean-looking man who had been chosen chief military officer for the new colony in America. John saluted smartly, even though his heart thudded against his ribs.

"What do *you* want, Smythe?" Standish gruffly demanded. "Can't you see I'm busy? The people are waiting to hear what our scouting party discovered. Step out of my way. I have to enlist volunteers for a longer exploration."

The corners of the captain's mouth turned down. "I suppose it will have to be after the Sabbath. Anyway, we have to find a place for our permanent settlement. I don't have time to waste standing here talking to you." Standish waved his hand, as if to brush John aside like a troublesome insect.

Pale November sunlight shone on John's short brown hair and danced in his bright brown eyes. His heart pounded even harder, but he did not back down from the captain or his cold stare. "I know, sir. That's why I stopped you. I want to go with the exploring party." John kept his gaze steady, without a single blink.

"You?" Standish laughed unpleasantly. "I need men, not lads. Try again in a few years, if we survive that long in this God-forsaken land." The corners of his mouth turned down. "We'll be lucky if any of us are alive by the end of next year."

"Sir, I am almost thirteen," John persisted, even though refusal plainly showed in the captain's cold eyes. "I'm strong. I can also outrun every boy and most of the men on board ship." He flexed his right arm and grinned.

Captain Standish planted his feet apart, his hands on his hips. He gave John a sour, unconvinced look. "You're a cocky one, aren't you? I thought you Separatists were taught it's a sin to boast."

"Is it boasting if you know you can do something well?" John asked. "I only told you because I thought you might need a swift runner to carry messages."

A reluctant smile crossed the captain's hard face. He looked

John over from the top of his head to the tips of his worn boots. "Hmm. You are tall for your age. Wiry, too." He hesitated and tilted his head to one side. "I might be able to use you, at that." Standish drew his brows together in a ferocious scowl. "Very well. You may go if your father agrees and—"

"He plans to volunteer." John clapped his hand over his mouth. How had he dared let his burning desire to go ashore make him interrupt?

"Quiet, whelp!" Standish roared. "If you go, you are under my command. You will obey my orders, keep your mouth shut, and stay close to your father. Understand me?"

"Yes, sir," John mumbled. His face felt hot. For the first time during the conversation, he shifted his gaze and stared at the deck.

"Dismissed." The captain, shoulders back, spine straight and stiff as a musket, marched toward the group of people eagerly awaiting his report.

"Thank you, sir." John clapped one hand over his mouth, this time to hold back a whoop of glee. Now if Father would only let him go!

John followed Captain Standish. He pretended he was stalking a deer in the forests and stepped lightly, so his footsteps would make no sound. When they reached the waiting crowd, the captain marched to the front of the little band. John squirmed his way in next to his father, an older edition of himself.

Mother and almost-eleven-year-old Sarah stood with the

women. Petite Sarah's green eyes looked enormous in her freckled face. Curly wisps from her dark brown braids peeked out from beneath the hood of her cloak. Mother also had green eyes, but her braids were wound on top of her head. She gave John a smile.

John shuffled his feet uneasily. How would Mother feel about him going with the men? And Sarah! He rolled his eyes. Even though he gave his sister less to worry about now than when they were in Holland, Sarah was bound to tease him to stay behind. "Why worry about that?" he muttered, so low no one around him could hear. "First, I must get Father's permission."

John remained silent, although he longed to clutch his father's arm and plead to be taken ashore with the other volunteers. He just *had* to go with the second scouting party. When the first band of sixteen men set off in the longboat, John had ached to be one of them. It would be more than he could bear to be left behind again!

Captain Standish barked, "I know you're all waiting to hear what those of us who first stepped foot on the New World discovered in the brief time we were ashore. We saw no signs of habitation. The sandhills here are similar to the downs in Holland but better and wooded. We suspect there are miles of forests. We saw an abundance of oak and sassafras, pine and juniper. We saw birch and holly, some walnut and ash. Near the swamps are cedar and red maple."

His dour face brightened. "Although we didn't find any

good water, we dug into the earth. It is rich, black, and good for planting."

A murmur of approval swept through the crowd. The first sight of the rocky coast had been less than promising. Rich, black earth meant abundant crops.

Father laid an arm across John's shoulders. His eyes glistened. His thin, strong face glowed with hope, so strong it settled deeply into John's heart. When Father looked like this, surely nothing too bad could happen.

"I suppose it is too much to ask that any of you Separatists will consent to be part of an exploring party until Monday," Standish said. The trace of a sneer twisted his face.

"Monday will be time enough," Governor John Carver quietly told him. "Tomorrow will be given over to preaching, praise, and prayer, as is our custom. Monday we will begin our work." His lips twitched. "My wife, Katherine, and the other women are eager to wash clothes. Did you find a place suitable for such a long-postponed purpose?"

"Yes. There is a small pond not far away. The water isn't good for drinking, but it will serve well for washing."

"Good. While the women and girls are scrubbing the stink of the voyage from our clothing, we men will separate into groups." Governor Carver looked over their number. "I suggest that those who are too sick to be among the exploring party use the time searching for food."

"I agree." Captain Standish took charge once more. "Smythe," he said, looking at Father, "if you consent to go with me, bring your son. He may prove useful, if he can live up to his boasting as to speed!" Loud laughter came from the group of people, then several men stepped forward to volunteer, Father among them.

John clutched at his father's rough coat. "Please, may I go?" He held his breath and clenched his free hand until the nails bit into his sweaty palm.

Father looked him over, much as Myles Standish had done earlier. This second inspection made John feel he'd been measured inside as well as out.

"I see no reason why not, especially as Captain Standish has requested it." A twinkle lurked in his eyes, but his mouth stayed solemn. "How is it that he knows so much of your running skills? And what is this about boasting?"

John felt his face turn dark red from embarrassment. "Uh, I didn't know whether he knew I could run fast, so I told him. I didn't think it was wrong to do so, when God has given me long legs that have learned to travel swiftly."

"I see." Father folded his arms across his chest and grinned. In that moment, his expression was almost identical to John's. Father beckoned to Mother and Sarah, who came at once. "Well, shall we let this son of ours go?"

Perfect trust showed in Mother's eyes. "So long as he promises to stay close beside you," she agreed.

Before John could holler with delight, Sarah asked, "Why must you go? There are plenty of men. I know you're almost a man, but you don't know how to fire a musket. What would happen if you crossed paths with a bear or wolf? What good would you be to the scouting party?"

"If Captain Standish thinks I am man enough to go, I am, Sarah Smythe. Oh, what's the use? You're a girl, and girls are always afraid!" John knew he was being unfair when he said it, but he couldn't chance having Father change his mind.

"That is enough, John." Father's smile vanished. "Your mother was a girl herself not long ago, and I don't know any man braver than she. Did you not see how she cared for the sick and weathered the hardest storms on the Atlantic without a word of complaint?"

Father's hand lightly touched Mother's shoulder, then came to rest on Sarah's head. "This one is just like her. There is no fear for herself in your sister. Only for you, and with just cause. In the past, you have been careless and fallen into trouble. Sarah has truly been her brother's keeper. It is well for you to remember this and show her more respect."

Father's stinging criticism made John feel ashamed. And guilty. A hundred times Sarah had kept silent about things he did that would upset Father and Mother.

"I'm sorry," he told her. "Forgive me?" Inspiration struck him. "If I find any curious or pretty things ashore, I will fill my pockets for you."

Sarah rewarded him with a smile. "Thank you, but be careful, please."

"I will." John added with a sigh, "I only wish we could go tomorrow and not have to wait until Monday."

"Explore on the Sabbath?" Sarah's eyes opened wide. "You sound like a heathen." She proudly raised her chin. "Elder Brewster says we must always set a good example for the crew, the London Strangers, and the Indians. What kind of example would it be to have you go tearing off on the Lord's Day?"

"She is right," Mother put in. "It is God's own commandment. 'Remember the Sabbath day, to keep it holy. Six days shalt thou labour, and do all thy work; But the seventh day is the Sabbath of the Lord thy God. . . . For in six days the Lord made heaven and earth, the sea, and all that in them is, and rested the seventh day.'"

"Mother, why did God need to rest?" Sarah asked. Her forehead wrinkled. "I wouldn't think God would ever get tired."

"I have always felt God set aside that time to simply appreciate and enjoy all the beautiful things He created," Mother said. A little smile played about her lips. "He also set an example for us. So did Jesus. Setting aside one day out of every seven to remember Him and spend time being glad for all He has given us is not too much to ask, is it?"

"No, Mother."

John squirmed, thinking of the endless services they held each week. Many times in Holland, he and Sarah had envied the Dutch children, especially on Sunday. The Dutch boys and girls laughed and sang and played games just outside the church door. The deaconess who sat with the Separatist children in a special section watched them with a sharp eye.

A few times John and Sarah had forgotten the strict rules against talking and laughing. The deaconess promptly boxed their ears. One time she whipped John with a birch rod. When they weren't listening to sermons or singing hymns on Sundays, John and Sarah were expected to sit quietly.

"I don't understand how it can be wrong to be joyful," John had complained to Sarah more than once. "God must have been happy when He finished His world." Now John secretly sighed. He loved God. Yet how could he live through another long, long Sunday knowing that on Monday he'd step onto the shores of the New World, land of freedom?

CHAPTER 2
A Cry for Help

To Sarah's joy and John's dismay, the scouting party from the *Mayflower* did not go on Monday after all. While the women and girls washed clothes in the small oval pond, small children ran on the sands. How good it felt to be out in the fresh air after the long days and nights huddled in their smelly quarters!

Some of the men walked the beach. Excitement spread when

they found mussels and clams. For nine weeks, the travelers had been without fresh food. The Pilgrims had never seen clams or mussels before and didn't know anything about eating them. Many of them stuffed themselves and ended up sick. Fortunately, Father and Mother cautioned John and Sarah not to be greedy. They escaped the stomach upsets that followed.

Meanwhile, carpenters examined pieces of the damaged shallop. "Sorry," they told Governor Carver and Captain Standish. "The boat has been battered so badly it will take us some time to get it ready for use."

Standish scowled. John knew the captain hated for things to come up and make him change his plans. The disappointed boy secretly sympathized with him. Surely the new military leader was as eager to explore the New World as John himself!

Tuesday passed with John so impatient he worked off his extra energy by racing up and down the deck. A cold Wednesday morning dawned. Standish, privately called "Captain Shrimp" by some, called his volunteers together and announced, "We will go on foot." He glanced south toward what appeared to be the mouth of a river, then shook his head. "That can come later. For now, we will go northeast." He strutted to the head of the scouting party. "Muskets ready?"

"Ready," came the answer. John looked at the gun his father carried. Only this morning he had watched Captain Standish demonstrate how to use a musket for the benefit of those who didn't know. It took time to load. First, Standish poured black powder down the muzzle and then tamped and wadded it. Next, he dropped in a lead ball and shoved it down with a thick pad. When the captain completed his preparations and released the trigger, John was startled by a yard-long burst of flame, a deafening roar, and a cloud of smoke.

"Mercy!" Sarah, who had hidden behind her brother in order to see without being seen, jumped a foot off the deck. "If it takes all that time to get ready, why won't the Indians or bears or deer already be gone?"

John secretly wondered the same thing but didn't want to admit it, so he just grunted. He knew it didn't fool Sarah and felt glad when she slipped away after giving him a knowing look.

John soon forgot everything except the fact that he was actually going exploring. He longed to follow directly behind Myles Standish but set his lips and fell into step at the end of the line, close behind his father. One false move and the captain would order the youngest member of the party to return to the *Mayflower*.

The next moment, a gruff voice said from in back of John, "Step lively, lad. I'm right b'hind ye."

John turned. A wide grin spread over his face. The big sailor Klaus who once had threatened to feed John to the fish if he didn't stay away from the rail of the *Mayflower* trudged along in the rear. "I didn't expect to see *you* here," John said.

"Came t'see the New World, didn't I?" Klaus snapped, face grim as ever. Only a flicker of light in his small dark eyes showed the friendship he felt for John.

"Aye, aye, sir." John laughed from sheer excitement.

"Button yer lip," Klaus warned. "If Cap'n Standish heers ye, it'll be back t'the ship fer ye, I'm thinkin'."

John realized the wisdom of his friend's advice but couldn't help whispering, "I'm glad you came along." He eyed the wicked knife stuck in Klaus's belt and the way the seaman rested one hand on its hilt. He had fought pirates and had a long scar on his shoulder to prove it. If they ran into unfriendly Indians, Klaus would be a good man to have with them.

"Face for'ard, now. Keep yer ears open an' yer mouth shut," Klaus hissed.

John did as he was told.

A quarter of a mile they marched. A half mile. Three quarters. A mile. The corners of John's mouth turned down. Where was the glorious adventure he had expected? There wasn't anything exciting about walking the beach. Where were the Indians? For all the signs of life here, the explorers might as well be in the middle of the Atlantic Ocean.

"Halt!" Captain Standish's command stopped John in his tracks.

"Indians," someone whispered.

Indians! John and the rest of his party stared. A handful of dark-skinned people and a dog were coming down the beach toward them! John felt his heart leap. Were they friendly? The barking dog certainly wasn't! It danced around while the Indians stared, pointed, and chattered among themselves. The dog snarled and made short charges toward the white men, then followed the Indians when they turned and raced up the sandy beach.

"After them!" Standish commanded.

John's feet automatically carried him forward with the others, but his mouth went drier than when he ate salty fish. What if twenty, fifty, a hundred more Indians lay in ambush, just waiting for the scouting party to chase the small group? What match would the untrained Pilgrims be on the Indians' land, where they knew every thicket and hiding place?

John plowed on through the sand. His breath came in gasps. Far ahead, the Indians and dog grew smaller and smaller, until at last they were out of sight. Captain Standish slowed the pace but ordered his followers to keep on.

They followed the tracks made by the Indians for miles, but without any luck. Night shadows stole across the land. At last, the party gave up their search.

"Tomorrow we will find them," Standish said.

"Of course we will," others heartily agreed. "We need to speak with them and find out if they are part of a larger party."

John wasn't so sure they could catch up with the Indians. He wasn't even sure he wanted to catch them. Or the snarling dog. It was a whole lot easier being brave while talking about the Indians than when standing on an unprotected stretch of beach with night coming on! But then, who was he to argue with Captain Standish, Governor Carver, William Bradford, and the others who were older and wiser?

He glanced at his father and saw doubt. The expression on Klaus's face showed he wasn't any more convinced than John, but the sailor only grunted. John wanted to laugh. He didn't dare. It still wasn't too late for Captain Shrimp to send him packing!

It didn't take long to make a fire and camp. Standish ordered sentries to stand guard. John slept restlessly and awakened a short time later. What was that noise? He lifted his head and peered about but saw nothing.

Whoosh. Whee. It came again, an ominous grumbling, followed by a strange whistle.

John sank back in place. He stuffed a chunk of blanket in his mouth to keep from laughing and waking up the sleeping men. The frightening sound was Klaus, flat on his back at John's left hand, snoring like a banshee!

When the boy got control of himself, he nudged Klaus. The sailor muttered in his sleep and turned on his side. Again the night became dark and still. John peered up at a few stars that glimmered between the clouds. Why should he be afraid? Sentries stood guard. Father slept on one side of him, Klaus on the other. Another gale of laughter threatened and passed. Peace crept over John. Even more important, his heavenly Father kept watch, no matter how long and dark the night around them might be.

Movement in the sleeping circle of men made John aware

he wasn't the only restless sleeper. Some mumbled. Another tossed and turned. John grinned and decided he could think about the Indians in the morning. He stared at the stars until they blurred, then fell asleep again, secure in the knowledge he was protected.

No other disturbances broke the night. Early the next morning, the explorers took up the trail. "Surely there is an Indian village nearby," someone said.

Captain Standish was his usual unpleasant self. "That's your opinion," he said in a voice sour enough to curdle milk. "We'll only know that if or when we find it, now won't we." He straightened his shoulders and pranced down the beach ahead of the others.

The speaker fell silent. John felt glad he hadn't been the one to be reprimanded. So far he'd managed to stay as far from their leader as possible.

A little later, they discovered a wide creek. Standish halted the men and looked away from the water toward the woods. "The Indians went that way," he said.

How could he know? John wondered. He tried hard to see tracks but found none. In a short time, he forgot everything except how miserable he felt. Thorny thickets clutched at his hands, head, feet, and clothing. He was so thirsty that his mouth and tongue felt like dry sandpaper. Would they ever get out of the woods and find water to drink?

"I'll wager the Indians are hidden not far off, laughing at us," he grumbled, trying to pull free of yet another thorny branch.

Klaus said something in a language John didn't understand. It was probably just as well. The seaman could curse in several languages. A reluctant grin crossed John's hot, sweaty face. At least Klaus didn't say bad things in English—not when the Separatists were around. Some of the crew did, even in front of the women and girls.

Too proud to call out for help, John carefully pried himself away from the branch, one thorn at a time. "Why did God have to make thorns, anyway?" he asked his father.

"There were none in the Garden of Eden," Father said. Sweat and drops of blood from a thorn he hadn't been able to duck dribbled down his face. "They came along with sin."

John stopped struggling for a moment. "Does the Bible say so?"

"The Bible says everything in the Garden of Eden was perfect until the tempter came," Father said. He laughed. "I wouldn't call these thorns perfect, would you, John?"

"Perfectly terrible," John replied and went back to his task.

At last all of the exploring party freed themselves. Tattered and torn, gasping with thirst, they rested for a time, knowing in minutes they must rise and continue on.

"We must have water soon," John whispered to Klaus, who plodded behind him as usual.

"Aye." Klaus licked his parched lips.

The word had barely left the burly seaman's lips when a terrified shout sounded through the woods.

"It's William Bradford!" John screamed. He leaped to his

21

feet and ran after Myles Standish, who had unsheathed his sword and was charging toward the spot from where the cry for help had come!

CHAPTER 3
Where are the Indians?

"Help! Somebody, help me!" William Bradford's voice sounded weak.

"Hold on, we're coming," Captain Standish bellowed. "Forward, men! Muskets ready. Make all the noise you can. Bradford's been captured by the Indians!" He brandished his sword and plunged deeper into the woods.

John Smythe put on a burst of speed. With Klaus muttering at his heels, the swiftly running boy passed the others of the party until he was close behind Myles Standish. His tongue felt thick with thirst and fear of what lay ahead. Yet he would not turn back or hide behind the others simply because he was the youngest of the party. He had boasted of being almost a man. This was the time to prove it.

Standish tore into a clearing and halted so quickly that John had to sidestep to avoid running into him. "Bradford, what have they done to you?" Standish roared.

John stared. Rubbed his eyes. Stared again.

A purple-faced William Bradford hung upside down before them. Both arms and one foot kicked wildly in the air. The other foot was securely caught in a noose attached to a bent tree! "Get me down," he croaked, swinging back and forth from his efforts to free himself.

A slash of Standish's sword cut the noose. Bradford tumbled to the ground.

"Where are the Indians?" the captain roared. "Where are the miserable wretches who did this to you?" He whirled, as if expecting to see Indians springing on the group of panting men who had gathered around him.

William Bradford took a deep breath. The purple left his face, only to be replaced with a dull red. "There aren't any Indians. I stepped in one of their cleverly set deer traps!"

"Well, I'll be—" Standish's mouth fell open.

No Indians? To John Smythe's horror, laughter bubbled up

inside. He mustn't laugh. Captain Standish's face had turned nearly as purple as Bradford's had been while dangling from the bent tree. Having a boy laugh would wound the captain's dignity and make him feel even more ridiculous than he already did.

"Excuse me," John gasped. He lunged into the woods away from the clearing, covering his mouth to keep from howling like the Indian dog. "No Indians," he choked out when he could no longer hold back laughter. "No Indians!" Now that he knew William Bradford was not injured, memory of him dangling from that noose was the funniest thing John had ever seen.

After being so scared, it felt good to be able to laugh. John knew he needed to return to the group, but he just couldn't stop laughing. Every time he tried, he remembered the scene and laughed some more, so hard that tears poured down his grimy face and left wet streaks. Finally John sat up and swiped at his eyes and hot face.

Klaus parted some bushes and walked toward him. For the first time since John had met him, the big seaman's face split in a grin so wide it stretched clean across his face. "If'n yer through carryin' on, I'm t'tell ye we be ready to go." A mighty guffaw came from the strong throat. "In all my sailin' the seven seas, I've never seen sich a sight. Ye'll be fer tellin' it to yer sister. Aye?"

"I can hardly wait!" John sprang up. "Sarah will think it is as funny as I do." He chuckled. "I don't know which was funnier: seeing William Bradford hanging there or the expression on Captain Shrim—Standish's face when he demanded to know where the Indians were!"

"Aye." Klaus chuckled again. "The Cap'n 'll be some time livin' this down." He cocked his head to one side. "Tell yer sister t'hold her tongue. I'm thinkin' 'twill be bad t'remind him."

The warning settled John down. He also remembered how thirsty he was. "I hope we find water soon."

"Ayc." Klaus led the way back to the others.

Standish eyed them suspiciously and said nothing. His usually red face showed an even darker color, but he merely said, "Bradford, can you travel?"

The victim of the deer snare nodded. "I'm a little stiff and sore, but all right, thank God." Bradford's lips twitched. "I must have been a pretty sight, hanging from the tree like a piece of moss!"

Except for the sour captain, the little party exploded, letting out all the laughter that had built up inside them. "Laugh while you may," the captain told them. "There will be little enough to be joyful about in the days to come."

His prediction dampened the high spirits of the scouting party. They silently fell in behind him and followed his lead.

At last they found water. John threw himself down beside the others and drank until he could hold no more. "Nothing ever tasted so good," he told his father. "Now I know why Jesus said we will be blessed if we give no more than a cup of cold water. I never appreciated what it meant until now."

Father wiped drops from his mouth. "We often take things

for granted until we must do without them," he quietly told his son, then stooped and drank again, as if he could never get enough.

Refreshed and with spirits rising, the explorers went on. They discovered they were on a neck of land. John could see water on both sides of them. Soon they came out onto the beach. Ahead stretched a clear, inviting pond. "Look," someone shouted. "A cleared field!"

Sure enough, the broad open stretch showed corn had once been planted there. Curious mounds of earth lay heaped up. At Captain Standish's command, his men opened one of the mounds. Everyone crowded close to see what it contained.

A bow, some old arrows, and a pile of bones lay before them. "Oh, no!" John felt the blood drain from his face. "We've dug into a *grave*!"

" 'Tis bad luck," Klaus solemnly announced. The only sign of fear John had ever seen in his friend's face appeared, and Klaus hastily backed away.

"It's sacrilege," others agreed. "Quick. Cover it up!" The diggers immediately replaced the earth and smoothed the mound, eager to get away.

"Do you think it was an Indian warrior?" John asked his father.

"Perhaps, since the bow and arrows were buried with the body. I understand that is an Indian custom."

John didn't have much time to think about it, for they soon discovered other things. First, they found the remains of an actual house. An enormous kettle lay nearby. So did a bunch of sand piles. The men looked at one another.

"What are they?" the explorers wondered. "Surely they cannot be more graves."

At the captain's orders, some of the men dug into the sand piles. John breathed a sigh of relief at what they found. "Corn!" he hollered. "Baskets filled with dried corn—some still in ears."

"Thank God," John Carver cried. "Fill the big kettle. Stuff your pockets full."

"The corn belongs to the Indians," John protested.

"Quiet, whelp!" Captain Standish scowled at the boy.

John couldn't hold his tongue. "But it's stealing! How can we expect the Indians to be friendly if we take what is theirs?"

"It is good that you are concerned, lad." Governor Carver smiled at John. "I promise that we will pay the Indians back in good measure and more. Right now, we must have the corn to keep our people from starving."

John thought of Sarah, so thin and pale from the voyage. He thought of himself, his stomach never filled because there wasn't enough food. His mouth watered. "Father?" he whispered.

"Do as we are commanded," Father said, reluctance in his eyes. "We must survive and will trust in God to help us make it right with the Indians."

Carrying the precious corn, the scouting party hurried over the dunes and back to the beach where the *Mayflower* waited.

They had been gone several days. Had anything happened while they were exploring?

John straightened his shoulders to better bear the weight of the corn stuffed in his pockets. He eagerly watched the men shoot off their muskets, knowing the signal would tell those on the *Mayflower* to launch the longboat and bring the returning party to the ship.

John's heart beat faster. He began to whistle. Wouldn't Sarah's eyes pop when he told her everything he had seen and heard on his first adventure in the New World!

Sarah Smythe had not been idle while her father and brother roamed the beach and forests. Always a good helper, she worked alongside Mother, scrubbing clothes and dirty blankets. She won approving looks and high praise from the other women for her hard work.

"Mercy, she is as good as a full-grown woman," some said. Mother only smiled, but the pride in her face made Sarah feel good. She thanked God that she was strong, in spite of being short and petite. She flew from task to task, green eyes shining and curly dark-brown braids tossing.

Sarah had another memory that she kept treasured in her heart, like a rare jewel in a box. It helped a lot during the anxious time of waiting for Father and John to return. Each time fear for their safety sneaked up and grabbed at her, Sarah whispered what Father had told John: *There is no fear for herself in your sister. Only for you. . . .*

Once Sarah asked her mother, "Do you think Father was right? About me, I mean. I don't really worry about me. Just about John."

"You are a loving sister," Mother said. "Any boy would be proud to have you care for him as you do John. Even though he teases you, always know how much he cares about you. You are also a joy to your father and me."

Sarah blushed until the red dimmed her freckles. "Mother, sometimes I wish I were John so I could go exploring, too. I want to see more of the New World than what we can from here, and I'm so tired of cleaning these smelly old blankets." She looked with loathing at a pile of blankets waiting to be washed. They were stiff from dried salt water and the vomit of sick passengers.

Mother's eyebrows raised, and Sarah hurried on. "I know it's silly. Goodness, John barely got to go, and he's a boy." She giggled. "Can you imagine what Captain Standish would look like if I begged to go scouting? I can just see him." Sarah placed her feet apart, squared her shoulders, and made fists of her hands. She put them on her hips, tucked her chin into her neck, and said in a deep, unnatural voice, "Begone with you! Girls are made for *tea* parties, not *exploring* parties!"

Mother's green eyes sparkled with fun. "Respect your elders, Sarah."

"I do. It's just that Captain Standish acts like he is more important than anyone else." Sarah dropped her imitation. A troubled look crossed her face. "He isn't a believer, is he?"

"Nay, but we pray he may become one of us." Mother sighed. "We must also appreciate what he is doing for us. Father says he feels Captain Standish will be faithful to his duties, no matter what happens."

"I'm sorry."

"As am I for laughing at your nonsense," Mother admitted.

Boom. Boom, boom, boom.

"The signal!" Sarah joyfully shouted. "The men are back!" She ran to the rail of the anchored *Mayflower* and shaded her eyes with one hand. "John promised to bring me whatever he found," she cried. "I wonder what it will be?" She caught sight of Klaus and moved back. Friend he might be, but the sailor's scowl when he caught her by the ship's rail still sent shivers through Sarah!

CHAPTER 4

A Midnight Howling

The moment John stepped foot on the deck of the *Mayflower*, Sarah ran to him. "I am so glad you are safe!"

He grinned at her. "Aren't you glad to see Father?"

"Of course I am," Sarah indignantly replied.

"You worry more about me, though, don't you?" John teased.

Her freckled nose went into the air. "With good reason." When he started to protest she said, "Never mind. What did you bring me?"

"Just you wait and see!" John's eyes sparkled, and his hands crept toward his pockets. "Hold out your hands and make a cup of them."

Sarah started to obey, then put her hands behind her back and demanded, "You won't give me something squishy like a worm, will you?"

"Where would I get a worm this time of year? C'mon, Sarah. You can trust me. Honest. Put your hands out and close your eyes."

Sarah slowly did as her brother asked. All the time he had been gone, she'd tried to think what he might find. Cones from the evergreen trees? Pretty shells? She felt a shower of small objects pour into her cupped palms, then something long and rough. Her eyes popped open. She looked at what she held. Dried corn. Kernels and an ear. "Oh, John!" she whispered. "It's the best present in the whole world." She wanted to hug him and dance, even though the Separatists permitted no such foolishness. Real corn, here, in her hands.

"Mother, just see what John has brought!" Sarah said when she could finally tear her gaze away from her gift.

"I know. Isn't it wonderful? William, how glad we are," Mother said to Father with a grateful look.

"I want to hear every single thing that happened," Sarah told John. "But first, we have some news for you. While you were gone, we had a visitor."

John, who had wearily dropped to a pallet on the floor, sat up straight. His eyes opened wide enough to satisfy even Sarah. "A visitor? Don't tell me an Indian came when we didn't see any except those first few we never could catch!" Disappointment spread over his face.

Sarah laughed. "I didn't say it was an Indian."

"There's no other ship in the harbor, and we're miles from any other white people." John looked puzzled. "Who else could it be? Did he come in a canoe?"

"No." Sarah giggled again. For once she had news before John. It was fun to keep him guessing.

"Then he must have walked," John figured out. "Is he still here?"

"He's still here, but he didn't walk." Sarah burst into laughter. So did Mother.

"Go ahead and tell him," Mother finally said.

"Susanna White had her baby," Sarah explained. "The first white child born in New England. Susanna and William named their new son Peregrine."

"Peregrine! I thought the Hopkins family had already chosen the worst possible name when they called their son Oceanus," John protested.

"It means Pilgrim or wanderer," Mother put in.

John grinned. "You were right, Sarah. He isn't an Indian. He didn't come in a canoe, he didn't walk, and he's still here. Now will you listen to what happened to us?"

"Of course." She scooted closer to John, propped her elbows on her knees and her chin in her hands, and prepared to hear John's and Father's adventures.

An hour later, John finally finished his exciting stories of everything that had happened on the trip. Sarah solemnly said, "I want to see the New World, but I *don't* want to get caught in a deer trap and hang upside down. Or be so thirsty I don't know what to do. Or have to fight my way out of thorn thickets. You and Father will be in danger whenever you go on one of those expeditions."

"God will protect us," John told her.

Sarah shook her head. "Not if you do foolish things. Stay close to Father."

"I have to." John made an awful face. "Captain Standish will have my hide if I don't. So will Klaus." He grinned. "That is, if Father doesn't get to me first!"

Sarah wasn't satisfied with the answer but didn't want to nag. She touched a torn place on her brother's jacket. "Tomorrow when it's lighter, I'll mend that for you."

"Thank you." John yawned. "I don't know when the next scouting party is going out. I hope I get to go along."

"Don't plan on it," Father warned. "I heard Captain Jones say he planned to lead the next party. I suspect it will be after the shallop is ready. Captain Jones wants to explore the river we saw close to where we found the kettle and the corn. The river's mouth is swampy, but it's wide enough for the shallop."

"Do you think Captain Standish might speak a good word for me?" John asked. Sarah noticed how round and anxious his eyes looked.

"Perhaps," Father said. His brown eyes twinkled. "I don't think he suspects you bolted into the woods to keep from laughing."

Father grinned and looked even more like John. "I have to admit it was a ridiculous sight, with William Bradford hanging by one foot and Myles Standish demanding to know where the Indians were! I doubt there were any for miles around. Those we saw acted more frightened of us than we were of them." He yawned. "It's been a long trip. Time to say goodnight."

Sarah lay wide-eyed and sleepless long after her family fell asleep. When she did close her eyes, visions of Indian graves, Indian corn, and Indian deer traps ran through her head.

"Father," she prayed. "You know I wish John would be happy just to stay on board the ship. He isn't, though. He will be terribly disappointed if he can't go again. Please keep him safe and help me to be brave." Comforted, Sarah fell into a deep and restful sleep.

Ten days later, the shallop was repaired enough for use, although more work needed to be done on it. Thirty men climbed aboard, but not John. Captain Jones chose those he wanted and scoffed at the idea a mere lad could be useful to him. "Stay here and protect the ship," Jones said.

John knew he was being mocked but was wise enough to know something else. Showing disappointment or arguing with the captain would merely strengthen the older man's opinion that John was too young to go.

"Aye, aye, sir." John put on as cheerful a grin as he could and saluted. The surprise in Captain Jones's face almost made up for not being part of the new exploring party.

"Good fer ye, lad," Klaus hissed in John's ear, before ambling down the deck in the rolling sailor's walk the crew used in order to stay upright during storms.

Father echoed the words. "Taking disappointment like a man is important," he told John. "Each time we do this, it makes us stronger for the next time." He glanced at the sky. "It may be well you were left behind, son. I don't like the looks of those clouds."

Father's fears proved correct. The scouting party ran into terrible weather. The shallop had to turn back. Some of the Pilgrims refused to do so. They waded through icy, waist-deep water to get to shore. Up hills and down valleys through six inches of snow they went. The wind blew. It snowed all that day and night, then froze. When they finally returned to the ship, many of them were so sick that they never recovered.

When the weather improved the scouting party tried again and found a few deserted wigwams, built of bent sapling trees with the ends stuck in the ground. Thick mats covered the wigwams both inside and out. A mat also covered the wide hole used as a chimney. Another mat made a low door. Even more mats served as beds.

The scouting party found wooden bowls, earthenware pots,

many baskets, deer feet and heads, eagle claws, and other curious things.

At Corn Hill, they dug in the frozen earth and discovered more corn to eat as well as seed corn and some beans. Again they vowed to pay the Indians for what they took and triumphantly carried their treasures back to the *Mayflower*.

"This is a real find," the leaders excitedly told the people when they returned to the ship. "Indian corn is well known by the explorers from the Caribbean and the Carolinas, as well as here. It gives two harvests a year and makes into good bread. We are fortunate, indeed, to have found it."

John wasn't sure how he felt about the corn. They needed the food desperately, but if they took the Indians' corn, what would the brown-skinned people do for food? He quickly put the worry out of his mind when the scouts reported they'd seen a plentiful supply of game: deer, partridges, wild geese, and ducks.

Edward Winslow described seeing whales in the bay. "One lay above water. We thought she was dead. One of the men shot, to see if she would stir. His musket flew into pieces, both stock and barrel! Thanks be to God, no one was hurt, although many stood nearby. The whale gave a sniff and swam away."

Captain Jones and others more experienced in fishing decided they would try whaling the next winter. They could make three thousand to four thousand pounds in whale oil, a fortune indeed!

To John's delight, as soon as the shallop was completely

repaired, another expedition set out. This time Captain Standish was in charge. He took the same group that had gone with him on his earlier expedition. John waved goodbye to Mother and Sarah, then huddled between Father and Klaus. The cold was so intense that the spray froze on their coats. Two men fainted from the cold.

This would be no nearby expedition. Robert Coppin, who had been in New England before, knew of a better place to settle straight across the bay at Cape Cod. As evening approached, the shallop drew near shore.

"Look," someone cried.

The men could see about a dozen Indians on shore cutting up a large stranded blackfish. The scouting party watched the Indians dance about, then vanish into the woods.

John felt his mouth go dry. Would the Indians trouble them? He felt relieved when the shallop landed a good mile away to camp for the night. With strong arms, he eagerly helped the others gather logs and branches to make a crude stockade around them and their fire. When darkness fell, he could see the distant fire of the Indian camp, but night passed without any disturbance.

The next day, the group split up. One party took the shallop to explore the shore. Klaus, who hated walking unless it was on the pitching deck of a ship, went with them. The others went on foot. John's feet grew tired. He kept a sharp eye out for Indians but saw no sign of them except the remains of the fifteen-foot blackfish.

At sunset, the two parties met again. Again they barricaded themselves with a screen around their fire and went to sleep. About midnight a loud howling and the sentry's warning cry, "Arm! Arm!" brought John out of bed and to his feet. Men snatched their guns from their coats where they had put them to protect them from the damp. *Boom. Boom, boom* rang out into the night. The howling stopped.

"Wolves," Klaus grunted. "I heerd 'em in Newf'ndland. Go back t'sleep." It took time, but John finally settled down and fell into a restless sleep.

When the sky lightened, the men began repacking the shallop. An argument broke out. Some of the men wanted to keep their muskets down by the water until they were ready to leave. Others said the muskets should stay with the men. Because they couldn't agree, some of the men came up the hill to breakfast unarmed.

Without warning, the same horrible howling heard in the night rang out. Klaus bellowed, "Hit the deck, lad; that's no wolves!" He threw John to the ground with one mighty arm, snatched his wicked knife from his belt, and crouched protectively over the stunned boy.

A storm of arrows hissed through the camp!

CHAPTER 5

A Day to Remember

Ssssss. Thud. A man leaped the barricade and screamed, "Indians! Indians! They're shooting arrows at us!"

John could see nothing from his uncomfortable position on the ground except Klaus's knees, one on each side of him. He could hear, though. The terrifying hiss of the arrows, their sickening thuds when they slammed into the barricade, were beyond his wildest imagining. The awful howling continued.

Suddenly Klaus sprang to his feet with a yell. Fighting fear, John scrambled up. A horrifying scene met his eyes. Two of the scouting party with muskets fired, then frantically reloaded. Two more stood by the entrance of the barricade, waiting for the opportunity to make their fire count. Others, wearing armor and carrying short, curved swords, fled to the creek for their guns.

The Indians tried to cut them off. One big attacker fearlessly stood behind a tree and let arrows fly as fast as he could fit them to his bow. Once, twice, three times, the Pilgrims shot at him. The Indian didn't budge.

Myles Standish took careful aim. John forgot the danger and watched in fascination. *Thwack! Zing!* The Captain's shot sent great splinters of wood and bark flying from the tree, all about the man's head. With a shriek, the Indian retreated, zigzagging through the trees for cover against the shots of the explorers. The others of the raiding party immediately followed.

"After them, men!" Standish ordered. "We'll prove to those cowards we aren't afraid of them!" The men chased the Indians, Klaus among them. They fired a few more shots, then returned, full of boasting.

"We showed those savages," a man yelled. "I'll wager they will think twice before they attack us again!" A roar of approval sounded.

Captain Standish cut in, his voice colder than the winter day.

"I'll wager you had better think twice before you lay down your muskets and have to face the enemy unarmed again."

The celebration abruptly ceased. John noticed resentment on the faces of those who didn't like taking orders from Captain Shrimp. It didn't speak well for the rest of the trip. Unwillingness to follow a leader could mean trouble.

"Is anyone hurt?" Standish barked.

"Nay, not a man, but just look at that!" Governor Carver said.

John looked in the direction the governor pointed and gasped. Arrows lay on the ground. Others stuck clean through some of the coats the men had left hanging on the barricade. A cry of anger went up, but Governor Carver soberly reminded them, "We can be thankful no one was hurt or killed. Let us give thanks." He knelt on the ground. So did everyone else.

"Praises be to Thy name, Almighty God. We thank Thee for Thy mercy in delivering us from the hands of the enemy this day," Governor Carver prayed. John added his own silent prayer of thanks.

When the prayers ended, John and the others picked up all the arrows they could find. "May I keep one?" he asked his father.

"I don't see why not." Father gave John a comradely grin. "I doubt that either Mother or Sarah will want one as a souvenir!"

Klaus grunted, but John laughed out loud and hurried to help finish packing the shallop. He climbed aboard with the others, and they set out again.

Several hours later, snow and rain began pelting down on the open boat and its miserable passengers. A screeching wind turned the sea into a raging torrent. By mid-afternoon, the waves grew so high, the explorers knew they must find a safe harbor.

Crack! The rudder snapped. A murmur of fear swept through the boat. Klaus snatched an oar, thrust it into a sailor's hand, caught up a second, and began to row with powerful strokes.

"Be of good cheer," Robert Coppin shouted. "I can see the shore." Yet the strong sailors' combined strength barely managed to steer the wildly tossing craft. John knew better than to bother his friend with questions or fears. Klaus's sweat-streaked face and heaving shoulders showed his struggle against the greedy sea.

Above the roar of the storm came the sound of cracking. "The mast has broken into three pieces!" Captain Standish bawled. John watched in horror as the sail hurled into the sea. He stared at the great rocks straight ahead. Only the hand of God could save them now.

Just when he knew they would crash and be torn to bits by the rocks and pounding waves, the rowers managed to change course. In the gathering gloom, they brought the shallop into quieter water.

"I have made a terrible mistake," William Coppin cried. "The Lord be merciful to us! My eyes have never seen this place before. The master mate and I would have run us ashore in a cove full of breakers."

The valiant sailor who was helping Klaus steer took command. "If you are men, row like fury and put about, or we shall all be cast away! There's a fair sound before us. I doubt not we shall find one place or another where we might ride in safety."

Somehow, in spite of the pitch-black, ferocious night, they limped into the sheltered side of a small island.

"Shall we stay on the boat, in case there are Indians here?" someone asked.

Chilled to the bone by the rain and drenching ocean spray, John shuddered at the suggestion. So did others. "We'll take our chances with the Indians," they decided. "We'll all die from the wet and cold if we don't build a fire." A group including John, his father, and Klaus stumbled to shore. The weary, freezing band took what felt like forever to get a fire going, then huddled close to the blaze. About midnight, the rest of the party joined them. The wind had shifted, and the ground froze hard.

John couldn't sleep, even after his teeth stopped chattering. What a day! First, the Indian attack. Then, one of the worst storms he had seen. Would he ever forget the sickening sounds of arrows or of the rudder and mast breaking? No. Neither would he forget the debt everyone aboard the shallop owed Klaus and the other brave sailor who had fought the screaming storm—and won.

The next day was the Sabbath. To everyone's great relief, it dawned sunny and calm. There were no Indians on the island. The exhausted explorers dried everything in front of the fires and cleaned their guns. They also thanked and praised God for bringing them through the storm.

That Monday, serious explorations began. The men repaired the shallop so that it was sea-worthy. Then they sounded the harbor and found it fit for shipping and a good place for the *Mayflower* to anchor. They investigated the mainland and discovered many cornfields and little running brooks. Although it wasn't ideal, it did appear to be the best spot available to set up a permanent home.

"Men, let us return to our families and friends," Governor Carver said.

"Yes, indeed," William Bradford quietly agreed. The look of worry caused by his wife's poor health and discouragement had carved deep lines in his face. He looked much older than his thirty-one years. Three of the company had already died at Provincetown Harbor, and William Bradford feared his wife would not make it through the long, hard winter.

John felt sorry for William Bradford, who had given up so much to become a Pilgrim. Did he ever long for England, for the uncles and aunts who had raised him after his parents' death? John wondered, *How would I feel if Father and Mother died? Or Sarah?* He swallowed hard. Except for the mercy of God, he and Father would have drowned in the terrible storm, leaving Mother and Sarah alone and sad in the New World.

Suddenly John wanted to see the rest of his family more

than anything in the world. He loved going adventuring but desperately wished to be back on the *Mayflower*.

He thought about the Indian arrow he had carefully packed inside his blankets. Perhaps he should make light of the attack and not worry his sister and mother. A pang at not being able to tell them all the exciting details went through him, but he shrugged. There were plenty of other things to tell, such as the good news that in a few short days, the *Mayflower* would sail to their new home.

"I wonder if anything interesting happened while we were gone," John asked Klaus when the shallop finally got back to the *Mayflower*. "Last time, Peregrine White was born."

"Aye." Klaus stared at the ship riding at anchor in Provincetown Harbor. He scowled, and his voice sounded uneasy. " 'Tis uncommon quiet, I be thinkin'."

It was quiet. Too quiet. With all John's squinting, he couldn't see a single Separatist on the deck—only Captain Jones and members of the crew who had stayed on board the *Mayflower*.

" 'Tain't Indians," Klaus muttered. "Cap'n and the crew're too peaceable."

John didn't answer. Something was terribly wrong. He felt it in his bones, as Captain Jones sometimes called it. Dread held him back when he wanted to board ship and find Mother and Sarah. Not until Klaus clambered aboard and held down a strong hand did John step foot on the *Mayflower*, wishing he weren't there, not knowing why he felt that way.

"I wonder where our womenfolk are?" Father's puzzled

look showed he didn't understand why they weren't there to greet the returning party. He headed for the sleeping quarters, with John just behind him. The sound of weeping floated up from the crowded area long before they reached it.

"Mother? Sarah?" John blinked and tried to adjust his eyes to the dim light.

"Here." A woebegone face peered at him from a corner. "Oh, John, the awfulest thing has happened!"

He ran to Sarah and flung himself down beside her. "Not Mother!" The terror he had felt during the Indian attack and the storm was nothing compared with this.

"I am fine, son." His mother's muffled voice started his blood flowing again.

Father dropped to his knees next to Mother. "What is it, Abigail?"

John had to lean close to hear the words that fell like hailstones. "Dorothy Bradford has drowned."

"It can't be true!" John's chest felt tight. He remembered how William Bradford had looked just a short while earlier, anxious and eager to get back to the ship. "How did it happen?"

"A tragic accident." Mother sounded as if she had wept so many tears there were no more left in her. "Apparently, she fell overboard when no one was around to hear her cries and save her." She took a deep breath. "John, take your sister on deck and tell her about your journey. I wish to speak with your father."

"Of course." He stood and helped Sarah up. As soon as they were topside, John peered into Sarah's tear-stained face and asked, "Why is Mother acting so strange? She isn't like herself at all."

Sarah looked both ways. She gulped and twisted her apron front into ugly wrinkled knots but said nothing.

"What's the big secret?" he demanded.

She fearfully looked at him. "Promise you won't tell? Mother doesn't know I heard her talking with some of the other women. I don't believe it, anyway!"

"Don't believe *what*?" John felt his patience slipping, in spite of how miserable his sister looked. Even her braids hung crooked.

Sarah stood on tiptoe and whispered in his ear. "Some people are saying Dorothy Bradford's drowning *wasn't an accident*!"

Chapter 6
More Trouble

John jerked back from his sister so quickly she nearly lost her balance. "Sarah Smythe, what did you say?"

"Shh!" She placed a finger over her lips and leaned close again. "Some of the people say Dorothy Bradford did not drown from an accident."

"You don't mean somebody *pushed* her?" The thought made him sick. "Impossible!"

"No, but it's just as bad." Fresh tears came to Sarah's eyes. "They say she leaped into the sea, that she hates it here and went crazy because she won't ever see her little son in Holland, and—"

"It's wicked gossip, and I don't believe a word of it!" John cried, keeping his voice low. "She was only twenty-three years old. I know she's been sick, but so have a lot of others." His stomach churned, and he felt like a heavy rock lay in the bottom of it. "Mother doesn't think it's true, does she?"

"Nay, son." Father had come up to them so quietly that neither had heard him. "Neither do I. This is a sad thing, and the least said about it, the better. William Bradford will need all our friendship. Don't mention his wife to him. He has already shown he prefers silence in the matter." Father put an arm around each of them. "Mother and I are counting on you to be loyal."

"What if people talk to us about it?" Sarah asked.

"Simply tell them you have been asked not to speak of it." He sighed and looked across the bay. "Only ninety-nine of our number will sail to our new home. God grant that we do not lose many more."

Long after Father went below, the children stayed on deck. John quietly told Sarah that there had been a storm and the explorers had seen some Indians. He quickly described the area where they would settle. Sarah asked a few questions, and then they fell silent. Neither made any attempt to seek out friends, even Klaus. They had known Dorothy Bradford since

51

they were small. They still found it hard to believe the frail, white-faced woman had drowned.

"It will be many months before the news travels across the ocean," John said at last. He thought of Holland where a small boy waited for a mother who would never come back to him. His eyes stung. *Please, God,* John silently prayed. *Take care of William Bradford and his little son. John is his only child. Keep him safe.*

"John?" Sarah asked quietly. "How can people who don't believe in God stand it when someone they know and care about dies?"

"I don't know." Her brother stared out into the growing darkness. "We feel sad enough even though we know we will see them again in heaven." He fiercely added, "It will be a lot better place than this! Just think of it, Sarah. God and Jesus will be there, and no one will ever get sick or die again. Or be hungry."

Sarah pulled her cloak closer around her. "If Father or Mother die, how will we find them when we go to heaven?"

"Don't worry about it. They aren't going to die for a long, long time," John told her. *I hope,* he added under his breath.

"They're lots older than we are, so they probably will die first," Sarah said.

"I never thought much about it." John paused. After a minute or so, he brightened up and told her, "I know! Father and Mother love Jesus more than anything, even us." He rushed on without waiting for an answer. "All we have to do when we go is look for Jesus. They'll be right by His side."

"It's getting dark, and we have to go below," John said, changing the subject. "I wonder how long it will be until we set sail?" He started to tell her he hoped they wouldn't run into the kind of storm the scouting party had experienced, but thought better of it. Why worry about something that might never happen? Besides, the *Mayflower* was far better equipped to deal with raging seas than the open shallop.

That Friday, four days after the return of the explorers, the ship hauled up its anchor and sailed into the bay. Neither John nor Sarah looked back at Provincetown Harbor. The spot held too much sadness. Strong head winds slowed the *Mayflower's* progress. It took until Saturday to cover roughly thirty miles across the bay. The ship anchored about a mile and a half from shore because the water was shallow.

A foot of snow lay on the ground. Women shivered and stood close to their husbands and children. Children stared round-eyed. "We shall continue to live on board ship until we build shelters," Governor Carver announced. "It will be necessary to take people and cargo ashore in the smaller boats."

Captain Jones looked sour. Klaus had told John and Sarah that Jones wanted to get the Pilgrims off his ship as soon as possible. "Tired o' yer comp'ny, he be, an' wants t'save his vittles," Klaus said.

Now the children exchanged delighted glances. Their friend Klaus would remain with them, at least for a time.

The Sabbath passed in the usual manner, with prayers,

Psalms, and praise. On Monday a band of armed men marched away to explore. John wasn't included this time but listened eagerly to their report when they returned.

"It's a good land," one said. "The soil looks promising. Great sections are already cleared. There are signs that huge corn fields once existed, although they don't appear to have been planted for at least a year. It looks like the Indians just up and abandoned them for no reason at all."

John couldn't help asking, "Why would they do that?"

A puzzled look crossed the speaker's face, and he rubbed his bearded chin. "Your guess is as good as mine, lad."

Another man eagerly put in, "We discovered berry bushes, timber, clay, and gravel. There is a high hill well suited to the building of a fort. From it, we can see the harbor and the country all around. It's ideal for defense, with a place for our cannon. We also found a clear running stream of good water."

Governor Carver looked around the assembly. "What more can we ask for than already-cleared land, sweet water, and a fine view of the surrounding area?" He hesitated and spread his arms wide. "We are ill prepared to meet the many challenges of this land. Yet we have all that is needed."

His voice rang out, and he counted on his fingers. "One, faith: in Almighty God and in ourselves. Two, courage. Did we not cross an ocean known for claiming ships and passengers? Three, good sense. Four, determination. Here, by the grace of God, we will build our colony, our home, and call it New Plymouth."

Mighty cheers rose from the company, John and Sarah's among them.

Governor Carver immediately ordered twenty of the strongest men to go ashore in the shallop and begin cutting wood. This time John wasn't disappointed at all that he had to stay on ship. A wild storm blew in. The anchored *Mayflower* tossed violently. The waves were so high the shallop could not get back. Those in the woodcutting party found themselves marooned and miserable for a few days.

One day, Sarah and Mother were mending clothes with the other women when Mary Allerton gasped.

Mother gave her a knowing look. "Is it time?" she asked.

"Aye," said Mary.

"Quick, Sarah," Mother instructed. "Run down to the main room and clear out a corner for us. Tell anyone who asks that it's time for Mary's baby to be born. Then get a bucket of water and some clean rags." Without waiting for an answer, Mother quickly turned to one of the other women, asking her to help get Mary safely down the ship's ladder.

Sarah hurried to obey Mother. As soon as the other passengers understood what was happening, they created a private corner for Mary. One of the men went off to let Isaac Allerton know his wife was about to give birth.

When Sarah returned with the water and rags, it was clear that Mother was worried. Something wasn't right. Sarah stood beside Mary and wiped the young woman's face with a cool cloth. The birth seemed to be taking forever. Finally, a beautiful baby was born, but it never opened its eyes or took a breath.

As Mary hugged her lifeless baby and cried, Sarah quietly stroked Mary's back, trying to comfort her. Everyone had been looking forward to the birth of another baby. But instead of feeling joy, they were now full of sorrow.

Soon, Christmas Day came. The Pilgrims considered Christmas a pagan holiday and did not celebrate it, but the others on ship had a small feast which they invited the Pilgrims to share.

Knowing the weather would soon become even colder, people worked harder than ever. Some cut trees. Others split the logs. The first thing to be built was a twenty-foot-square "common house" to store tools and house the workmen, then serve as a shelter for the sick and a church.

John and Sarah began to feel all they did was work, work, work. From before daylight until long after dark, there were jobs to be done. Everyone needed food and shelter. Muscles that had gotten little exercise during the months on the *Mayflower* quickly grew sore from the hard work.

"At least everyone being so busy keeps them from arguing and quarreling with each other," Sarah whispered to John one night.

He moved his sore shoulders and yawned. "That's 'cause if everyone doesn't work together, none of us will survive," he told her. "There are a few who complain about our leaders. They say they were better off under the king of England's rule than starving in America."

He sighed and rubbed his stomach. "I know we need to finish the common house, but how I wish some of us could go hunting or fishing! We'll have to wait until next year for ripe berries and fruit and nuts, but scouts say there's a lot of seafood and waterfowl." He licked his lips. "I'd give anything for the leg of a roasted duck."

"So would I." Sarah shifted position and rubbed her aching back. "I am tired, tired, tired. Sometimes I think if I have to carry another bucket of water for cooking, bathing, or washing clothes, I'll scream! I won't, though. Mother stays so cheerful and always has such a sweet smile, I can't complain to her. Just to you."

"That's good." John yawned again, opening his mouth so wide he wondered if he'd dislocated his jaw. "Father and Mother are working even harder than we are. Besides, what good would complaining do? The work still has to be done."

"It never ends." Sarah drooped. "When Mother and I aren't cooking and washing and mending clothing for our own family, we help those who are too sick from scurvy and pneumonia to take care of their families. There's no time to spin and weave cloth for more clothing."

She put a rough hand to her mouth to nurse a sore finger. "Ow! Making torches from pine logs leaves my hands full of splinters. We have to have something to see by, though. I can hardly wait for spring, so we can dip wicks into melted fat and make candles. We're also running low on soap." She made a face. "I hate making soap. It's so hot stirring the lye and fat in the big kettles over the fire."

"Poor Sarah." John opened his eyes enough to see the dark circles under her eyes. If only she didn't have to work so hard! Yet if everyone didn't do all that they could, their small group would never survive the winter.

Once the common house was built, families built their own homes. Father built a rude thatched hut that looked like an Indian lodge. Some of the settlers made dugout caves in the hillside. Single men lived with families to cut down on the need for houses, and plot sizes were determined by family sizes. New Plymouth was laid out in the shape of a cross to make it easier to defend. A sturdy stockade surrounded it.

John and Sarah soon learned how unforgiving their new home could be. Peter Browne and John Goodman took their dogs when they went to collect reeds for thatching. They didn't return that afternoon, so Myles Standish sent out a search party. No trace of the two men could be found.

That night, everyone in New Plymouth wondered where the two men were. The next day, the men returned and told their story. Their dogs had scared up a deer. Eager to bring in fresh meat, the two men followed. They got lost in the woods. Noises like the howling of wolves terrified them, and they wandered all night in the forest. John Goodman's shoes had to be cut off his frostbitten feet. He died a few days later.

When Sarah learned what had happened, she tried to be brave. Yet her eyes showed fear every time Father or John left

New Plymouth. The only way she could bear their leaving was to remind herself how much God loved them. Sarah felt sure John suspected her secret. He never said anything, but almost every time he returned, he brought her a cone, a curious shell, or a funny story. They made her feel a little better.

Then one cold night in the middle of January, the cry, "Fire! Fire!" echoed throughout New Plymouth. The Smythe family jumped from their sleeping mats and hurriedly put on more clothes. Even in the dim light of a pine torch, Sarah and John could see the terror on their parents' faces.

CHAPTER 7
Fire!

A dozen voices took up the cry. "Fire! The common house is on fire!"

John raced toward the building, more frightened than he had ever been in his life. The common house was filled with the sick, including William Bradford, who had collapsed while working, Governor Carver, and many others. "Please, God, help them!" John prayed.

Someone shouted words the running boy could not make out. Cries of terror came from the gathering crowd.

John put on a burst of speed, caught up with a man running in front of him, and frantically snatched at his rough sleeve. "What is it?"

"Gunpowder," the man panted. Sweat and fear covered his face. "Barrels of it. Some open. Stored in the common house!"

"No!" John's hand fell away. The new danger threatened not only those who lay ill, but all of New Plymouth. It was far more deadly than the flames that burned the common house's thatched roof and spread to its walls. If the fire ignited the gunpowder, it would explode.

"Here, boy!" A man coming toward him from the common house thrust a rude wooden bucket into his hands. "Fetch water, and be quick about it!"

The order released John from his horror. If ever the speed he knew God had given his long legs was needed, that time was now. He turned and raced for water. Would the spark that set the common house on fire destroy everything the Pilgrims had worked so hard to build? Would it claim victims from the rows of sick inside the burning building?

"God, save them!" John yelled, never slowing his pace. He filled the bucket and dashed back to the burning building, being careful not to spill the precious water. When he got there and passed the bucket to eager, waiting hands, a great sob of relief tore from his throat.

The barrels of gunpowder sat away from the common house, safe from harm.

"Who got the powder out?" John demanded of a breathless, soot-streaked man standing nearby and slapping at sparks on his clothing.

"God, I reckon." The man coughed. A river of tears poured down his grimy face. "I never saw such a thing." He coughed again. "Even the weakest among us somehow managed to help! They tottered up from their sick beds, grabbed those barrels as if they were feathers, and hauled them out."

He mopped at his face and put out a spark greedily burning yet another hole in his already-tattered garment. "We lost a lot of clothing we can ill afford to spare, but praise be to God, no one was killed, at least so far." A shadow darkened the speaker's face. As if suddenly aware of his own weakness, he slumped to the ground and lay there panting.

John bit his lip, understanding only too well what the man meant. The fire and gunpowder had been cheated of their victims. But from the looks of those who had staggered from the common house and stood shaking with chills, their efforts could bring more death to the settlers.

All through the night, John continued hauling buckets of water to the common house. Everyone was fighting the fire, but the people who were sick eventually collapsed in the snow. He noticed Mother and Sarah busy helping them get up and make their way to small homes where at least they could stay dry. Father was pouring water on the roofs of nearby homes to keep them from catching fire.

Finally, the fire was put out. As the tired group looked at the steaming roof, they knew even more work lay ahead. The roof needed to be repaired and the common house cleaned before the sick could return to their shelter.

John and Sarah looked at each other. As she wiped her nose with the handkerchief her Dutch friend Gretchen had given her so long ago, Sarah said, "John, don't you sometimes long to be back in Holland where at least we had time to play with friends?"

"Do I ever," John said. "And we weren't so tired or hungry either."

"Well," Sarah said with a determined voice, "we certainly can't go back now. And if we're going to survive, we need to keep working. I'd best go help Mother cook up some porridge for everyone."

John watched his sister with admiration and then turned to join a group of men who were going out to cut more thatches.

Sickness and death continued to haunt the colony. Sometimes John and Sarah hated the New World, with its cold and hunger. What good was it to be free, when so many people in the colony lay sick and helpless? How many more would they lose in this harsh land?

John and Sarah were sad when Captain Standish's wife, Rose, died, but they grew to admire the gruff captain as they saw him work among the sick with Elder Brewster. "After what I've seen him do," John confided to Sarah one day, "I'll never call him Captain Shrimp again."

The Smythe family was alarmed one morning when Sarah

woke up flushed with fever. Having seen so many people die, John was afraid his sister would be next. For days, he did everything he could to help Mother take care of Sarah. He even helped with the cooking and washing. "God, please help my sister get better," he prayed.

When Father, Mother, and John could no longer keep their eyes open, Klaus stayed at Sarah's side. His big hands proved surprisingly gentle as he wiped her hot face with a cloth dipped in cool water. He also managed to secretly bring her small portions of food. The family never asked, but they suspected Klaus saved it from his own rations.

Finally, Sarah was able to get up, although she was so weak she could barely walk across the room. Her green eyes looked enormous in her thin face, and her freckles stood out as if painted on her nose and cheeks.

The first afternoon she was able to sit up, she peppered John with questions about what had been happening. "At least there hasn't been any trouble with the Indians," she said.

John grunted. "Depends on what you call trouble. No one can leave any kind of tool lying around or it mysteriously disappears. One of our men went out for ducks and saw Indians coming this way. The men working in the forest left their tools and came back after their guns. When they got back, both Indians and tools had vanished."

The corners of his mouth turned down. "Now the Indians are getting bolder. One day they stole tools from some of our people who left them just long enough for the midday meal!"

"We need our tools or we can't cut wood and make crops," Sarah protested.

"Don't judge them too harshly," Mother told the children. "This was their land before we came."

"It's ours, now. The King gave it to us," John protested.

Mother sighed. "I wonder how we would have felt if someone came to our house in Holland and told us it no longer belonged to us."

"Elder Brewster said it's for their own good," Father spoke quietly. "He says when we tell the Indians about God and Jesus they will be happier."

When the Pilgrims who were still living aboard the *Mayflower* fell ill, Captain Jones insisted most of them be taken ashore. "I can't risk having my men take your sickness," he barked. "It's bad enough we couldn't leave and go back to England as we planned. We don't intend to get your tuberculosis and pneumonia."

Some of those who had been passengers on the *Mayflower* weren't much kinder.

"One man fixed meat a few times for a friend who said he would leave him everything," John whispered to Sarah. He knew Father and Mother didn't approve of telling tales, but he was so angry he just couldn't keep it to himself. "The man didn't die right away, and you know what?"

John clenched his hands into fists. "The man who was supposed to be his friend called the sick man an ungrateful cheat! He said he wouldn't fix him anything more. The sick man died that very night."

Sarah's mouth rounded into an *O*. "You mean some of our own people are acting this way? How can they, when we so badly need to help each other?"

"From fear." John sadly shook his head. "The crew on the *Mayflower* is said to be even worse. They snarl at one another like dogs. Klaus says they think they're all good fellows when they're well. But once sickness strikes, the healthy crew members absolutely refuse to help those who are ill. They are afraid to go in the cabins and risk infection."

"That's terrible," Sarah exclaimed.

"Well," John said, "at least one good thing happened. Remember the boatswain who never missed a chance to curse us and tell us how worthless we are?"

"How could I forget him?" Sarah rolled her eyes. "He was awful! He never said anything nice about any of us."

"He has now." John took in a deep breath. "The few people from our group who were allowed to remain on board the *Mayflower* are pitching in to help the sick crew members. Our people refuse to just let the sailors die. Hard as it is to believe, the same boatswain who couldn't stand us told our people before he died, 'You, I now see, show your love like Christians one to another, but we let one another lie and die like dogs.' Can you imagine that?"

Sarah blinked hard. "I'm glad, but I wish he had learned about Jesus."

"I do, too." John felt sadness shoot through him like a swiftly speeding arrow. "Not just him, but all the others. More than half the crew is dead. I don't know if any of them knew Jesus." A great lump came to his throat. "I hope so." John took in a deep breath, held it, then slowly let it out. "Sarah, do you know what I want almost more than anything in the whole world?"

"Enough food to feel really full?" his sister asked and patted her flat stomach.

"More than that. More than anything except for you and Father and Mother not to die." John swallowed hard at the thought. There had already been too many deaths. Some whole families were wiped out, although no girls and only a few boys had died.

"What do you want, John?" Sarah asked.

"To have Klaus know Jesus. I think maybe he's starting to. When he told me about the boatswain he added, 'Somethin' fer a man t'think about, how ye Pilgrims tuk keer o' the likes of the bo'sun.'"

"What did you say?" Sarah eagerly leaned forward.

John stared at her. "I told him it was 'cause that's what Jesus would do if He were here and folks were sick, even folks who cursed Him."

Sarah's face glowed with pride. "Good for you! I don't think I'd have had the courage to say that, but oh, I'm glad you did!"

"So am I." John grinned, the first real smile that had settled on his face since before Sarah got sick and worried them half to death.

"What did Klaus say then?"

"Nothing." The disappointment John felt when he talked with Klaus came back. "He just cocked his head to one side and raised a shaggy eyebrow like he does when he's tired of talking, and then he mumbled that he had to get back to work."

"Maybe he will think about it," Sarah comforted. She patted her brother's hand. "John, someday when you grow up, you might be a preacher, like Elder Brewster. You could, you know."

Her total faith made John feel better, but he shook his head. "I can't imagine being a preacher. A carpenter, maybe, or a fisherman, or explorer. Besides, you know you don't have to be a preacher to tell people about Jesus."

"Perhaps not, but you'd make a good one." Sarah's faith remained unshaken. "You told Klaus, didn't you?"

"I just wish he had said more," John told her.

The next day he wished it even harder, for Father brought terrible news. Klaus was violently ill and lay burning with fever and freezing with chills aboard the *Mayflower*. "I feel it's only fair to warn you he will probably die," Father sadly added, "although our people are doing everything they can for him."

"No!" Sarah cried. John just shut his lips, ran away by himself, and began to pray harder than he had prayed in his whole life.

CHAPTER 8
The Promise

For a full week, Klaus hung onto life with every ounce of his strength. Those who cared for him shook their heads and said he should have died days before. They marveled that a man so sick still lived.

For a full week, John, Sarah, and their parents prayed for the seaman. Rough and without polish, Klaus had proven himself to be their friend again and again. Sarah couldn't think of him without crying. She remembered the food he had brought her and wept bitter tears. "If he had eaten it instead of giving it to me, he might not be sick," she said.

"Hush, child." Mother's stern command shocked John. Their mother sometimes scolded him, but she seldom raised her voice to her obedient, even-tempered daughter. "Klaus chose to give you the food. Don't spoil his gift by feeling guilty. You know he would not want it so."

Sarah sniffled, and John sent her a weak smile. He longed to think of something to cheer her up, but he couldn't. How could anyone laugh or think of funny stories when Klaus and so many others lay close to death?

"Father, may I go see him?" the boy pleaded.

"You mustn't!" Sarah cried. "You could become sick and die!"

"He didn't let that stop him from coming when you were so sick," John reminded his sister.

Fresh horror sprang to her eyes. "Then he did catch it from me." She threw herself into her mother's lap. "It's my fault. It's all my fault!"

"Sarah Smythe, stop that this minute!" Father thundered. "I will not have you carrying on in this manner. It is unbecoming to a child of God. We have put Klaus in our heavenly Father's hands. It is not for us to place blame on ourselves or on others." His white, set face showed no trace of his usual kindly expression.

The children gasped. Father had never spoken to Sarah in that tone. She raised her tear-streaked face and stared at her father.

"It hurts me to have to speak to you this way, but I must." Father looked weary. "God has blessed you with a loving, tender heart. He sees and is pleased that you care when others are sick or in trouble. However, you need to remember something. God does not expect you to carry the burden of all the sins and hurts of the world on your small shoulders." A beautiful look crept into Father's face, and he stroked Sarah's tousled braids. "That's why Jesus came."

"Father is right," Mother said in a low tone. "Jesus took those burdens to the cross. Our part is simply to trust and serve Him. Don't fret, Sarah. It has taken your father and me many years to learn this."

Mother smiled at Father. "Many times, we still feel like we need to take a hand in whatever life brings—to control it—instead of waiting for God to do His perfect work, as He has commanded."

"We must learn to be patient," Father added. "The Bible tells us this over and over. The prophet Isaiah said, 'But they that wait upon the Lord shall renew their strength; they shall mount up with wings as eagles; they shall run, and not be weary; and they shall walk, and not faint.'"

"It's hard," John muttered.

Father lowered his voice and whispered mysteriously, "That's where the promise comes in."

"The promise?" The children's ears perked up. For a moment the excitement of a possible mystery took their thoughts away from death and dying.

"The Bible is filled with promises, such as in Psalm 23," Father told them.

"I know that," Sarah cried. "David said the Lord was his shepherd and would take care of him—"

"Even in the valley of the shadow of death," John quickly finished. "Is that the promise you meant?" He eagerly looked at Father.

"It's a good one, but not the one I was thinking about." A faraway look came into Father's eyes. "When your mother and I fled from England to Holland, we didn't know what would happen. What if we were stopped by the authorities, beaten, or put in jail? I could bear it for myself, but I felt I could not stand it if your mother suffered at the hands of King James and his men."

A look of gratitude came to his dark eyes when he looked at Mother. "I finally shared my struggles with your mother. She reminded me of the promise, a single verse. We claimed it as our own. It has kept us going all through the years. Each time life becomes unbearable, we repeat the Scripture."

"What is it?" Sarah and John shouted at the same time.

"In Paul's first letter to the Corinthians," Father said quietly, "the great apostle promises we shall never be given more than we can bear, and that God will make a way for us to escape."

"Always?" Sarah left her mother and crept into her father's welcoming arms.

"Always, Sarah." His face shadowed. "This doesn't mean God answers every prayer the way we think He should or that

He gives us all the things we ask for. It does mean He answers in the best way."

John felt his heart pound with fear. His throat felt dry. Surely the best way wasn't for Klaus to die without knowing Jesus! His nails dug into his hands. "Father, I just *have* to see Klaus," he choked out.

Father looked at John. Once more, John felt himself being carefully weighed. "Are you man enough to see your friend close to death, perhaps dying? To smell the poison that is taking lives? The stink of sickness that clings in spite of all those who are able to help can do?"

"I am." John raised his head and looked his father straight in the eye. "Haven't I already carried slops for those in the common house and helped clean up when they have been sick?"

"Aye, lad. So be it." Father gently put Sarah aside. "Come with me, but mind what you say." He paused. "Let the Spirit of God guard and guide your tongue."

John didn't fully understand what Father said, but he nodded anyway. They boarded the *Mayflower* and walked toward where Klaus lay. John gagged. The stench of sickness and death on the ship made him want to head for the rail.

"Oh, God," he whispered. "Help me." Taking small breaths in the hopes of keeping from heaving, he followed his father's sure steps down the deck he had so often walked with Klaus. Would they ever stride that deck together again?

"Klaus, it's William Smythe," Father said in a loud, clear

voice when they reached the tossing, turning man. The sea-man's restless fingers picked at the blanket on which they lay. He opened his eyes, but John knew he didn't recognize them.

Could this gray-faced man really be Klaus? It seemed impossible. Where had all his magnificent strength gone, his way of showing without a word he could control any situation?

It *was* Klaus, for the sick man turned eagerly toward the sound of Father's voice. A broken whisper came from between his parched lips. "Tell th' lad. . ."

"The lad? John? Tell him what, Klaus?" Father asked.

Klaus stared, but John knew the sailor didn't recognize Father. Klaus lifted a trembling hand to his mouth. "Tell th' lad. . ." He made a mighty effort to raise himself but fell back to his pallet, breathing heavily, moving his body as if seeking a comfortable spot to rest. Sweat clouded his face.

"Is he dying?" John's heart gave a mighty lurch.

"He's very close to it. Stay with him, and I'll fetch water."

One of the hardest things John ever had to do was sit with his friend while the seconds limped into minutes. He tried twice to speak but could not. At last he said, "Klaus, I'm here. So is Jesus."

A slight change came over the still figure. His breathing slowed, and his thrashing body grew quiet. John pressed his lips tight together. Was this the end?

"Keep talking to him, son," Father instructed as he placed a bucket on the floor and dipped a cloth into the cool water to bathe the seaman's face. "One of the workers just told me that ever since Klaus fell ill he has been repeating, 'Tell th' lad,' over and over. Let him know you hear him."

John leaned closer, being careful not to get in Father's way. "I'm here, Klaus. It's John. Remember all the things we did together? Remember the rail, and how you told Sarah and me you'd feed us to the fishes if we didn't stay back?"

John searched his mind for things that might help him reach his friend. Had Klaus already gone so far down into the deep, dark valley only God could help him?

"That's it!" John whispered. "Listen to me, Klaus." He placed his hands on the big man's shoulders and gently shook him. " 'Yea, though I walk through the valley of the shadow of death, I will fear no evil.' David said that. He knew God was with him and he didn't have to be afraid. You don't, either."

Klaus didn't open his eyes, but something in the way he turned his head in John's direction gave the boy hope. Again and again John repeated Psalm 23. Each time he came to the part about the valley of the shadow of death, Klaus quieted, until he lay like one dead.

At last John grew so hoarse, he could barely whisper. Father laid a hand on his shoulder. "Come. We have done all we can. Now he is in the Father's hands."

Despair filled John. Why hadn't God heard his prayer? If only he had come sooner! Perhaps Klaus would have asked Jesus to forgive and save him. He slowly stood, feeling like someone had kicked him in the stomach. "He's dead."

"No, John. Just sleeping."

A stubborn hope sprang up inside the boy's heart. "Will he live?"

Father shook his head. "I cannot say. I do know your words reached him and stilled his tossing and turning. Now all we can do is wait."

"Let me stay with him," John begged. "Mother and Sarah need you, but I can stay. It may be the last thing I can do for him."

"You know the risks." Father's keen gaze studied John's face.

John thought of those who had died, many who had fallen ill after caring for others. "Father, Klaus would do it for me."

Tears sprang to Father's face. "Aye. Stay then," he said in a low voice. "And don't forget that when we serve others, we serve our Master." He touched John's uncombed brown hair, and the boy felt he'd been given a blessing.

One of the strangest nights John would ever know began when Father left. Alone with the silent Klaus, he had time to think. Midnight came, followed by the early morning hours. "Our bodies are at our lowest point then," Father had warned before he wearily trudged away. "Then also comes the greatest danger of loved ones slipping from this world into the next."

Would that happen to Klaus? What had the sailor wanted to tell John so badly that even in his fever he continued to call out? Perhaps he had only wanted to say goodbye. Or to warn him to stay away from the ship's rail.

Yet there was another possibility, so wonderful the tired boy who silently kept watch felt fresh strength flow through him. What if, during the time of sickness Klaus had remembered what John had told him about Jesus? What if he had cried out to the Lord in his heart, asking to be forgiven and saved? Wouldn't he want the one who had told him about Jesus to know?

John scrunched up his knees, rested his elbows on them, and laid his head on his folded arms. "Please, God, I have to know." It took all his courage to add, "If it be Your will." He prayed it again. And again. Only this time he couldn't finish the prayer. His eyes closed. His breathing slowed. Head still resting on his arms, John slept.

A slight sound roused him. He opened his still-tired eyes and saw daylight. Oh, no! Some guard he was, sleeping the hours away instead of keeping watch. If he were a sentry posted outside the stockade, he would be severely punished.

John gritted his teeth, took a deep breath, and looked down at Klaus.

CHAPTER 9
You Can't Stop Me!

When John looked down at Klaus, he expected to see a corpse. Instead, the sailor's small eyes twinkled. The shadow of a grin touched his lips. He licked them and croaked in a hoarse, unnatural voice, "Ye stayed wi' me?"

"Yes." John felt his face explode into a grin. "Just last night, though."

"I be thinkin' yer a brave lad." Klaus laid one big paw on

John's sturdy hand. "Now git afore ye ketches the fever."

John knew better than to argue. "I'll come back later. You'll be better then." He stood and turned to go.

Klaus's low voice stopped him where he stood. "Mayhap, but no need t'fret if I ain't. That Friend o' yers, Jesus, fergive me." A look of wonder came into the sailor's face. "Me, who's sailed the seven seas an' done black things! An' all I had ta do was ask."

John knelt next to him. He grabbed Klaus's hand and squeezed it with all his young might. "This is the best present anyone ever gave me," he cried.

"Aye, aye, mate." Klaus smiled again. It softened his face until he looked like a different man. "I be chartin' a new course, now." Some of his old fierceness came back. "Didn't I tell ye t'run along? Git!"

John laughed at the scowl that no longer hid Klaus's tender heart. Klaus's eyes shone steady and true, showing how much he had already changed in the short time since he signed on with a new Master.

Proud to be the bearer of such good news, John raced to his family. "Now all he needs is rest and good food," he announced. A frown chased away his joy. "Where are we going to get it for him?"

Father smiled. His eyes glowed with happiness until they looked like the sea at its bluest. "Captain Standish is sending a few men for game," he told his excited son. "A good meat broth can help Klaus and the others."

"May I go?" John held his breath. Sometimes Myles Standish took him. At other times and for no particular reason, he grumpily ordered the boy to stay behind. To John's disgust, it turned out this was one of those times, just when he wanted to go the most! He bit his tongue to hold back hasty words. They would mean he'd be left out of future hunting parties. Yet disappointment burned inside when Father and two other men left with Captain Standish.

"I'm needed at the common house," Mother told John and Sarah. She put on her warm cloak and bonnet and told John, "Cheer up. I know it's hard being left behind, but next time you will probably get to go. Besides, after caring for Klaus last night, you need some rest." A moment later she disappeared, leaving a disheartened John with only Sarah for a companion. Father had told him not to go back to the *Mayflower*.

"Klaus asked you to stay away," Father said. "When I get back, I'll go see that all is well. I want to tell him how glad we all are over his decision to accept Jesus."

John sat and glared at Sarah, who had done nothing to deserve his ill will. "It's my duty to help Klaus," he said. "Besides, I'm tired of people thinking I'm only a child." A daring plan began to form in his mind. "Sarah, I'm going to show them. All of them!" He hastily collected the warmest clothing he owned.

"Where are you going?" she gasped. "Father told you to stay off the *Mayflower*. If you follow the hunting party, Captain Standish will fly into a rage and order you back. John, you're going to get in trouble. Well, I won't let you do it."

Sparks flew from her eyes. "I'm going right to the common house and tell Mother you're planning something you know you aren't supposed to do!"

John whirled around to face her. "If you do, I'll never forgive you!" A black scowl appeared on his face, but he quickly forced a smile. "C'mon, Sarah. You never tell on me, and I've been good for ever so long!"

"All the more reason you shouldn't disobey now," she told him. Yet some of the anger left her eyes.

John added layers of clothing. He carefully took down a musket from the rough wall of their home and went through the slow process of loading it. Sarah watched with anxious eyes. She heaved a sigh of relief when he finished. "Be careful," she warned.

"I will. I just want to be ready when I see a deer."

"Then you *are* going after the hunting party! John Smythe, you know what's going to happen. Father will be so upset with you, and what if you get lost? Remember what happened to John Goodman when he got lost in the woods? I'm not going to let you go!"

John knew everything Sarah said was true. It made him squirm, but he wouldn't back down. "I'm going, and you can't stop me," he told her. "We don't know that Father and the hunting party will find game. I might. Klaus needs broth, and later, he'll need the meat. So do we. You're so thin that when you stand sideways, you hardly cast a shadow!"

A faint giggle encouraged him. John went on. "Do you think Klaus would stay home with the women and children if we needed food? Don't be a goose, Sarah, and *don't* tell anyone."

Sarah's giggle changed to hurt. "You don't have to be so bossy and cross."

John felt ashamed. "Sorry, but this is something I have to do. Be a good girl, and just maybe we'll have venison stew for supper." He shouldered the long gun and started on his way, letting Sarah think he was going to catch up with the hunting party.

John had a bad moment at the gate. The sentry challenged him. "Who goes there? Oh, Smythe. The hunting party just left. They went that way." He pointed. "You'll have to stretch those long legs of yours if you want to catch them." A grin split his broad face. "From what I hear tell, you can do it, too!"

"Thanks." John shifted the weight of the musket and carefully didn't commit himself. He felt a little guilty at deceiving the guard but told his conscience that after all, he hadn't lied. Was it his fault the sentry took for granted he was one of the hunters? He was, in a way. He just wasn't one of today's party.

John followed the direction the guard had indicated until tall trees hid him from the sentry's sight. Again he felt guilty, but the last thing he needed was to make the man suspicious. If the guard knew John was going to hunt alone, he'd be sure to stop him. Then where would John be? Right back with the women and children and in disgrace with the entire colony.

A dim trail led off from the path taken by Standish and his men. John decided to follow it. A half-mile down the trail, he found deer tracks and droppings that looked no more than a few hours old. His excitement grew. Surely Father and the others would overlook his disobedience when he got back with all the meat he could carry.

"I'll have to figure out a way to hide it so animals and Indians don't find it before someone comes for the rest of the meat," he planned aloud.

Intent on tracking the deer and dreaming of how it would help Klaus and the others, John failed to notice the storm swooping toward him. Huge clouds joined others. Yet not until they hid the pale winter sun did John notice.

When he did, he shifted his gaze between the tracks and the sky a half-dozen times. Should he keep on? Deer sought shelter from bad weather. The one he'd been tracking might be just ahead, already hunched down in a bed beneath the trees to protect itself from the coming storm.

John plunged ahead, scanning both sides of the trail. No deer. "Might as well turn back," he muttered in disgust. "It's getting so dark I couldn't see a deer unless it jumped up in front of me, and then I probably couldn't kill it. Of all the days for a storm, it would have to be this one."

He turned and rapidly strode back down the trail the way he had come. The musket felt heavier now, almost as heavy as his spirits. Going home with meat was one thing. He did *not* look forward to arriving empty-handed!

How far had he come, anyway? With darkness falling so rapidly, John had no way to judge how long it had been since he had left the stockade. He stopped and stared. Funny. He didn't remember stepping over a downed log in the trail when he came this way. Now one blocked his path.

Suddenly John felt fear. He impatiently brushed it away. It was no time to get panicky. He'd probably taken the wrong fork back where the trail branched. He turned, retraced his footsteps, and tried the other path. It led directly to a huge, uprooted tree and ended.

Thoroughly confused, John went from one promising trail to another, only to become more hopelessly lost than ever. Worse, he stumbled and fell heavily. The musket flew out of his hands, and it was too dark to find it!

His body felt sweaty and cold by turns. The growing gloom soon hid any landmarks he might have recognized. All he could see in every direction was endless forest. The only way he could keep on the faint trail was to kick out with his legs. When they hit brush, he knew he had strayed.

John's stomach growled loudly, reminding him the last time he had eaten was too long ago. "Why didn't I bring some food?" he complained to a huge evergreen tree whose heavy branches bent almost to the ground. The rising, howling wind bit through his clothing. He stamped his feet.

"Guess I thought I could get a deer and be home before anyone but Sarah knew where I was. If I only had a fire! No chance of that without the musket." He waved his arms to warm himself. "I wonder what Father would do if he were caught out like this?"

Plop. A large wet drop fell from overhead onto John's upturned face. Plop, plop, plop. Others followed. From the looks of the angry clouds, an icy downpour was on its way.

John dove beneath the friendly, listening tree. Its overlapping branches grew so close together they protected him from the rain, but he knew his problem wasn't solved. Huddled against the rough tree trunk, he tried to think. He thought of asking God for help but hesitated. How eager would God be to rescue a boy from the misfortune he had brought on himself?

"I don't have a choice," he burst out. "No one knows where I am. I can't just stumble around in the dark. God, you helped Daniel in the lions' den, but he got *thrown* in. He didn't just walk in by himself."

John sighed. "I should have listened to Sarah. Forgive me, please, God. I sure can't help myself, and no one knows I'm here but You. Why didn't I tell Sarah what I had really planned?" An image of him walking in the direction the hunting party had taken, then deliberately changing course brought hot color to his face. How foolish! No wonder Captain Standish and Father didn't believe that he had become a man.

An eternity later, John awoke from an uneasy sleep, stiff and half frozen. The slight warmth afforded by the branches could not match the growing cold.

According to those who knew, the winter was milder than

usual, but it still meant night temperatures around freezing. What should he do?

Even the tossing storms of the wild Atlantic Ocean had not been able to drown out John's spirit of adventure. Now he bitterly regretted leaving the settlement without permission.

"I can't stay under here. I'm freezing." He jumped up and hit his head on a branch. "Ow!" Rubbing the sore spot, he went on talking to God and to himself. "If I walk to keep warm, I may be getting farther from the settlement, but what else can I do? God, I'm in an awful mess. Please, help me."

Something important teased at his tired brain, but he couldn't remember what it was. He concentrated. Hard. "That's it!" he shouted. "Thank You, God!"

John crawled from beneath the branches of the great tree, turned up the collar of his coat, hunched his shoulders against the wind, and started walking.

CHAPTER 10
Where is John?

Sarah sadly watched John march away. A curious feeling of trouble ahead for her brother made her regret her promise not to tell Mother where he was headed.

"He *has* been good," she tried to tell herself. "This is the first time in ages he's done something he knows he shouldn't. It's only because he loves Klaus so much and wants to help."

She sighed. "But I would feel better if I knew for sure that John found the hunting party. Then even if he got in trouble, I'd know he was safe."

Sarah stared into space, deciding what to do. With Mother, Father, and John busy helping the sick, she was responsible for most of the home chores. She had more than enough work to get done that afternoon without worrying about John. Suddenly a smile crossed her face. She reached for her cloak that was hanging on a peg by the door and quickly stepped outside. With hurried steps, she headed toward the sentry.

"Where be ye off to in such a hurry, little Miss Sarah?" asked the guard.

"I was wondering if you saw my brother, John," Sarah said.

"Aye, he left a few minutes ago to catch up with the hunting party. With those long legs of his, he's probably with them right now. Did you need to get a message to him?"

"Oh, no," Sarah said, a relieved smile crossing her face. "I just wasn't sure if he had left yet. Thank you for your help."

With a nod of her head, she turned back to the small hut Father had built for their family. Removing her cloak, she quickly began catching up on her work.

Sarah and John slept in a loft above the one main room where the family cooked and lived. Each night the children climbed a ladder and slept on beds made from straw mattresses on the floor. Now Sarah climbed up to the loft to shake the mattresses and smooth them out. She also tidied the sheets, blankets, and rugs they had brought from England. They never put the rugs on the earth floor. Instead, they kept them on the beds for added warmth.

Scrambling downstairs again, Sarah shook out Father and Mother's straw mattresses. As soon as he had time, Father would make rope springs so they could have better beds, but Sarah wished they could some day have featherbeds. The linen bags filled with goose feathers made soft mattresses in summer and warm coverlets in winter.

"I should be thankful for what we have," she told the warm room. Father had laid wooden boards across two wooden sawhorses for their table. At night, he put the boards against the wall to make room for the mattresses. They had no chairs. Father always said, "When there is only one chair in a household, the man sits in it while his wife and children stand. I cannot be like them. Nay. John and I shall make a bench and we will all sit together. One day we shall have enough chairs for all."

A quick glance at the fireplace that provided light, warmth, and a place to cook showed it needed wood. The corners of Sarah's mouth turned down. It *always* needed wood. Sometimes she felt the fireplace was a greedy beast that sulked when she didn't feed it enough. The thought made her laugh, a pleasant sound in the small room. How hard they had worked to gather their wood! She and Mother picked up fallen branches. John and Father split and sawed. The whole family had carried the split wood to their home and built a great mound just outside the rough wooden door.

After Sarah had added wood to the fire, she straightened the everyday clothing hanging on wooden pegs on the wall. Their Sabbath clothing lay in a chest, along with extra bedclothes. Mother often warned them about being careful of their clothes. What they had brought with them would have to last for a long, long time.

Sarah giggled. "How it can, I'm sure I don't know! I've grown an inch since we left Holland and John's almost three inches taller. It's a good thing Mother and I put big hems in my dresses and made John's clothes extra big."

Sarah was so involved in her work that she didn't notice how late it was getting. A sharp gust of wind at the corner of the hut reminded her. She ran outside.

An army of storm clouds played tag across the sky. Sarah shivered from the cold. "At least John had sense enough not to go off hunting by himself," she whispered. "Surely the hunting party will start for home when they see the scowling sky." Yet honesty forced her to admit that in the deep woods, the men might not notice how dark it was getting.

Sarah shook her head and went back inside. She stood by the fireplace to get warm and wondered if Father and John would return before the storm hit. Memories of John Goodman dying so soon after he got lost in the woods troubled Sarah. But what could she do?

"I can pray," Sarah told the crackling fire. She plopped down on her knees before the blazing fire.

"Dear God, please be with John and Father and the other

men. John did wrong to run after the hunting party, but You know how much he wanted to help our friend. Thank You for helping Klaus. Thank You most of all that he knows Jesus." Sarah stayed on her knees for a long time, and when she got up, she felt better. Now if only John and Father would come home soon!

"Be a good girl, and we may just have venison stew for supper," John had promised. Sarah's mouth watered. Yet as each minute passed, a cold knot of fear grew in the pit of her stomach. Three times she wrapped up in her cloak, went outdoors, and peered into the worsening storm. No sign of John or of the hunting party.

Again and again she wondered what to do. Another hour went by. Sarah's smile had long since vanished. She continued to wait for her father and brother, a prayer on her lips, fear in her heart.

At last, Mother arrived, rosy-faced and chilled. "Ah, that is good, child!" She hung her wet cloak on the peg closest to the fireplace and held her hands out to warm them. "Where is John?"

Sarah hesitated. She would not lie, but the faint hope that John would come soon made her say, "I don't know. He went out but wouldn't say where he was going." *All true,* she told herself. *I just hope Mother doesn't ask when he left.*

"You don't think he would disobey Father and go aboard the *Mayflower* against orders, do you?" Mother looked worried.

Sarah shook her head until her curly braids bounced. "I

don't think so. He wanted to go and complained a bit, but I'm sure he wouldn't actually do that. Mother, is Klaus really, truly going to get well?" Her voice trembled.

"I don't know." Mother turned around so the fire could warm her back. Her green eyes looked troubled. "He is still a very sick man. We can only trust that God will take care of him in the best way. Daughter, even if Klaus leaves us, we know it will only be for a short time." She held out her arms and Sarah ran into their warm circle. "When we meet again, we will be together forever."

"I know," the tender-hearted girl whispered. "It's just that so many people have died." Her arms tightened around her mother. If only she could hold her close and keep her safe from sickness and death. She longed to tell Mother that each time someone died, the fear of losing her or Father got worse.

Be brave, she told herself. *It would worry Mother even more if she knew how you felt. She probably already suspects, but as long as you don't say it out loud, she can't know for sure. Mother has enough to think about without worrying over you.*

Mother sat down on the bench John and Father had made, pulling Sarah down beside her. Shadows from the fire flickered on her tired face. "Life is hard here, harder than any of us imagined." Her eyes glistened, and Sarah knew she was close to tears. "I do all I can, knowing the next time I go to the common house, one or more will be missing."

Sarah had never felt closer to Mother. "Why do our men

bury the dead at night?" she asked in a low voice.

Mother held Sarah so close the girl could hear the steady beat of her mother's heart. "We dare not let the Indians know how many of our people have died," Mother said huskily. "Once they realize our numbers are small and that we are so weak, they may become bold enough to attack."

Sarah and Mother silently huddled together on the bench until a sound came above the storm. "It's John!" Sarah felt weak with relief. She sprang up and flung wide the door. Father entered, empty-handed and with a set look on his face, but there was no sign of John. A furious blast of wind sent a cloud of smoke from the fire through the hut.

Father slammed the door shut. "We found no game, but at least we got home before the worst of the storm." He smiled at his wife and daughter, but only with his lips. His eyes held no hint of their usual sparkle. "I'll change into dry clothing." He shrugged out of his wet coat and looked around. "Where's John?"

"Isn't he with you?" Sarah asked, fear filling her heart.

"With me? Why would he be with me? You know Captain Standish didn't want John in our hunting party today."

"But John left and the sentry said he was headed toward the hunting party," Sarah explained.

"Left?" Father's eyebrows met in a frown. "When?"

"He went a long time ago. He said he was going to get a deer so Klaus would have broth, and—"

"You mean John is somewhere out in this storm?" Father's

93

face turned whiter than snow. "Abigail, did you know about this?"

"Nay. I knew he was upset over Klaus and being left behind by Captain Standish." She turned to Sarah. "How could you let him go?"

"I tried to stop him!" Sarah cried. "I threatened to tell you, but John said that if we needed food, nothing would keep Klaus from getting it for us. He said he *had* to go, that it was something he had to do. I even checked with the sentry and he said John had joined the hunting party." She covered her face with her apron and burst into sobs. "I'm so tired of trying to be a brother's keeper! John won't listen to me, and I get blamed for what he does!"

Shocked silence filled the hut. Sarah cried harder. How could she have spoken to Mother and Father like that, even if it wasn't fair for her to have to bear the burden of John's mischief?

"Daughter, I spoke too hastily," Mother said.

"As did I." Father picked Sarah up and hugged her. "We know your brother can be a trial, and you are to be praised for your love and patience. We also appreciate how much you have grown up. Although you are loyal and wish to protect John, you no longer allow him to lead you astray. It is not your fault he is rebellious. You cannot change John. All you can do is continue to set a good example. John must decide for himself how he will behave. Forgive us, Sarah."

The humbleness in Father's voice made Sarah feel better. "I

. . .it's all right. I know you are worried. So am I." She buried her face in her father's shoulder. "I've waited and prayed and waited and prayed all afternoon."

Father set her down. "I'll get a few neighbors and see if I can find him." He put his wet coat back on and slipped outside.

The waiting went on, and Mother tried to help time pass quickly by having Sarah eat some food. Less than an hour later, Father returned. "The storm has increased. We can do nothing until morning," he said heavily. "Sarah, go on up to bed."

She reluctantly obeyed, feeling Father had things to say to Mother he didn't want her to hear. For once her curiosity matched John's. When she reached the loft, she crouched near the top of the ladder. Spying it might be, but she could never sleep without knowing what Father had to say. She had to listen hard, but she did manage to catch his words,

"I pray to God the rain doesn't wash out John's tracks. I also pray John is wise enough to remember what he's been taught, which is to find cover and stay there. If he wanders around, it will make our search a lot harder."

Sarah crept to her bed and buried herself in her blankets under the rug. She lay sleepless, praying for her brother until the first rays of light crept into the sky.

CHAPTER 11
Left. Right. Left. Right.

Left. Right. Left. Right. John Smythe swung his arms and walked. Cold, hungry, and miserable, he wanted to run but dared not. His head throbbed, a painful reminder to keep a steady pace. If he crashed into a low-hanging branch, it could knock him senseless. He might freeze to death before he recovered.

Left. Right. It was getting harder now. How could a person keep going when his legs felt weaker than water? Could he starve to death in just one night? "Don't be a goose," he ordered himself. Goose. Oh, yes. He had told Sarah not to be a goose. Why must she fuss every time he struck out on his own? Yet if he had listened to his sister, he wouldn't be walking for hours and getting nowhere.

"Have to keep moving," John mumbled. "Klaus needs broth. Meat." He was so tired. Perhaps he should stop his endless marching and rest.

"No!" The sound of his own sharp cry alerted John to the dangerous state into which he had fallen. He scrubbed at his eyes. "I can't stop." Every horrible story he'd heard of those who rested and never woke up again haunted him. The stories also kept him walking long after he felt he could not keep on.

Left. Right. Left. Right. Was he going mad? John laughed wildly. Dangerous or not, he had to stop. "I won't sit down," he panted. He leaned against a tree trunk to catch his breath. If he closed his eyes for just a moment, would sleep keep them shut? He couldn't chance it.

Left. Right. On and on and on. Was this how a beast of burden who walked in a circle turning a mill wheel felt? He leaned against a tree once more. What were Father and Mother and Sarah doing right now? Would he ever see them again?

The thought jerked John out of his numbness. He saw more clearly than ever before how much pain his carelessness could bring to others. "God, if I died of sickness, it would be hard enough for my family," he cried. "If I die because I disobeyed and thought I was smarter than the hunters, it will be worse.

Pride goes before a fall. No, that's not it." He tried to remember. Father had certainly quoted it to him often enough!

"Oh, yes. 'Pride goeth before destruction, and an haughty spirit before a fall.' "

Shame spread through him. He'd pranced out of the stockade, sure he could find a deer even when Captain Standish, Father, and the others might not. All because of foolish pride. He had told Sarah he wanted to get meat for Klaus. It was true. He had also told her he intended to show everyone. Bitter regret for the anger that had sent him hunting shot through every part of John's body.

Left. Right. Left. Right. His feet felt like two anchors, weighing him down when he must keep moving. "God, forgive me," he whispered.

What felt like a lifetime later, John knew he couldn't walk another step. He leaned against a tree, as he had been forced to do so many times throughout the long, dark night. His eyes closed. He felt the rough bark of the tree on his hands when he slid to the ground. The pain pulled him back, and he opened his eyes.

Light. Blessed, wonderful light, showing morning had come at last. John got to his feet, so stiff and sore every muscle protested. "Thank You, God!" he shouted so loud a bird in a nearby bush answered him back. The growl of his hollow stomach reminded him he still wasn't out of danger. New Plymouth lay somewhere in the distance, and he still didn't know which way.

Now he must make the most important decision of his life, one that could well mean life or death. Everything in him screamed *go* except a single tiny voice that whispered *stay*. "No one will find me here," John argued. Yet the little voice won, partly because of his weariness. As weak as he was from lack of food, John realized that if he got even more tangled in the woods, Father would never be able to find him.

A new thought came, turning his predicament into a nightmare. What if Father and the other hunters didn't return home for several days? Sarah wouldn't worry about him because she'd assume he was with the hunters. The sentry would assume the same thing. "Please, God. Let someone know that I'm lost out here."

In spite of all his good intentions, John again slid to the ground. This time, his exhausted body refused to get up.

"John?"

The sleeping boy stirred restlessly. "God, is that You?"

"John." The cry came again. Strange. It sounded like Father. What was he doing in heaven? Or were they all back in Holland? Had everything been a dream: the *Mayflower*, Klaus, the terrible night of walking in the woods? John struggled to understand. When a third cry came, he shouted, "Here. I'm here."

His shout came out as a whisper that wouldn't carry a foot beyond where he lay.

"Son, where are you?"

A prayer went up from John's heart. *God, give me strength.*

He forced his eyes open, painfully got to his feet, and called, "Father?" It came out louder this time. John swallowed, then screamed at the top of his lungs, "Father, I'm here!"

A crashing of brush and heavy, thudding footsteps told him he had been heard. He sagged with relief. A heartbeat later, Father burst into view. Like a well-placed arrow Father raced straight to his target and gathered John in his arms.

The others of the rescue party followed close behind. "How'd you manage to keep from freezing?" one wanted to know.

"I prayed," John said. "Then I remembered a story I heard about someone just like me. He got trapped by a blizzard and didn't have any food or a way to make a fire. He knew he had to keep walking or freeze but couldn't see where he was going. Neither could I, so I did what he did." John stopped for breath.

"What was that, son?" Father quickly asked. His arms tightened, sending warmth through the shivering boy.

"I walked around the tree all night. It kept me warm, and I didn't wander any farther from the settlement." John yawned.

After a moment of stunned silence, relieved laughter came from the rescue party. One man slapped his leg, chuckled, and said, "Well, I never! Smythe, that's mighty clever."

John's heart thumped. "It wasn't me. I believe God made me think of the story." He looked at the men's faces. Some looked convinced. Others did not.

"I still say it's mighty clever," the man said again, but Father quietly added, "If John had done as he was told, he wouldn't have been in trouble at all."

"That's right, lad. Listen to your father from now on."

"I will." John looked at the ground. "I guess this is my last hunting expedition for a long time."

"It could have been your last forever," Father reminded him. "Now, let's get you home where you belong. There you will stay until you learn to act like a man instead of a child who goes running off when he doesn't get his own way."

John knew he deserved everything Father said, but it hurt to be corrected in front of the men. He also knew Captain Standish's judgment would be far harsher than Father's. Well, he'd take it like a man. He would never forget what could have happened to him without the love of God to protect and help him.

Afterward, John didn't remember much of the trip home. At one point someone spotted John's musket and rescued it from the snow, but John barely noticed. One weary step after another, he managed to keep going until just outside the settlement. *Left. Right.*

When the stockade gate swung open, John's knees buckled. Father slung him over his shoulder and carried him. If John hadn't been so tired and disgusted with himself, he'd have been embarrassed to be hauled home like a sack of grain.

His mind cleared. What would Mother and Sarah say? For one cowardly instant, he wished he were back in the forest. Better to face wild animals and storms and Indians than four green eyes that looked deep inside him and didn't like what they saw!

Father took him inside. "Abigail, Sarah, the lad is safe and unharmed. He needs food and rest. Bring warm, dry clothes and broth. We'll talk later." The last things John remembered were feeling the ice inside him melt when he drank the broth and then his father's strong arms helping him up the ladder to his bed.

John awakened to pitch darkness. Had he only dreamed that Father and the others had come for him? He cautiously shifted his body. The straw in his mattress crackled, telling him he was safely home. He turned over and fell asleep again.

The next time John woke, daylight had come. He slid farther under his covers. Dread of what the day would bring hung over him like a flock of screaming sea birds. Captain Standish would certainly kill any hope of future hunting expeditions. Others in the colony would scornfully point at the boy who wanted to be a man but sneaked off like a sulky child.

"I can bear that," John whispered into the still air. "What I hate worst of all is the way Mother and Sarah will look at me." His still-tired mind raced. "Or maybe they will just think it's about what they can expect from me." The thought cut deep.

"John. Sarah. Dress and come down quickly," Father's ragged voice called.

An uneasy feeling that had nothing to do with well-deserved punishment slowly washed over the boy. Muscles stiff and aching from his night in the forest, John managed to get into his clothes and down the ladder. He ran to the fireplace and warmed his cold hands at the blaze. Its cheerful glow felt good, but even the fire could not melt the icy fear that trapped John.

Mother's lips trembled. Sadness lined Father's face when he said, "Children, you must be brave."

For once, John didn't get angry at being called a child. "What is it?" He clenched his hands until he felt the nails bite deep into his palms.

"Word just came from the *Mayflower*. Our friend Klaus died in the night."

Sarah buried her face in Mother's big apron.

John fell back, unable to believe what he had just heard. "No," he said hoarsely. "No, no, *no!* Klaus was getting better. You know he was. That's why I went for the deer. He *couldn't* have died. It must be another crew member." He started for the door.

Father caught him halfway there. "Running isn't going to help."

"Let me go!" John twisted and turned. "It isn't true." A horrible thought pounded into his brain like waves against the rocky coast. "Did he know I was lost?" When Father blankly looked at him, John shouted, "That's it, isn't it? He knew and tried to come for me. *What have I done?*"

"Stop this, John." Father shook his son, not hard, but enough to get his attention. His eyes blazed. "You had nothing to do with Klaus's death. Plague took him, as it has taken many others and will take more. Klaus never knew you were missing." Father pulled John to him in a big hug.

John fought back hot tears, wishing he were a child again and could weep in his father's arms.

Father's hold tightened. "We grieve, yet we praise Almighty God that our friend met Jesus, our Savior, before it was too late. The bearer of the news said Klaus died with a smile on his face, and the words, 'Tell th' lad,' on his lips."

A great sob tore free from John's throat in spite of all he could do to be brave. He jerked from Father's arms, bolted up the ladder, and threw himself on his bed. A long time later, a small hand crept into his. In the dimness of the loft he saw Sarah.

"I loved him, too," she whispered. "I didn't even get to tell him goodbye."

John put his arms around his sister and rested his chin on the top of her head. Perhaps later words of comfort would come for Sarah, for him. Right now just knowing they still had Father, Mother, and each other helped. His mouth went dry with fear. All he and Sarah could do was cling to the promise that God would never send more than they could stand, but would always make a way of escape.

CHAPTER 12

What is a Samoset?

Sarah Smythe trotted alongside her tall brother and looked up into his face, her eyes twinkling. They had just come from Sunday meeting, and Father and Mother were walking ahead of them. "My, that was a good sermon." She giggled, then clapped her hand to her mouth and quickly looked around to make sure no one had heard her laughing on the Sabbath. "Elder Brewster's Scripture was about you."

John stopped dead still. "Whatever are you talking about?"

"The Scripture," Sarah patiently repeated. Her green eyes twinkled with fun. "Weren't you listening?"

"Not very well," John confessed. He stared at the *May-flower*, feeling the same ache that came each time he saw the ship where Klaus had died.

"You should have been," Sarah told him. "It just fits the way you are now."

Curiosity took John's attention from his sad thoughts. "Really? What Scripture was it? What did it say?"

"First Corinthians, chapter 13, verse 11." She smothered another giggle, and her face lit up with fun. "You know. The one where Paul says when he was a child, he spoke and understood as a child, but when he became a man—"

"He put away childish things," John soberly finished for her. "Do you really think I'm like that?"

"Oh, yes." Her cap-covered braids bobbed up and down. "You're ever so much more grown up. You're kinder to me, and I heard Father tell Mother he was proud of the way you took your punishment like a man."

She slid her hand into the crook his elbow made. "Father said even when Captain Standish roared like the wind, you held your tongue and looked straight at him. Mother's awf'lly proud. So am I." She hesitated, then whispered. "God must be proud, too."

"I hope so." John scuffed his boot on the hard ground. "I'm trying."

"I know," she said sympathetically. After a few moments of silence she added, "Tell me again what Klaus said the last time you saw him."

The ghost of a grin tipped John's lips up in the old way. "First he told me to 'git afore ye ketch the fever.' "

"That sounds like him!" Sarah chuckled. "What did he say after that?"

John had no need to search his memory. The parting with his friend stayed as clear as when it took place.

"I promised to come back later when he was better. Klaus said, 'Mayhap, but no need t'fret if I ain't. That Friend o' yers, Jesus, fergive me.' " John spoke in an exact imitation of Klaus. "He had a. . .a kind of beautiful, shiny look, if you can imagine. It made me forget the sickness and death and stink. Then he said, 'Me, who's sailed the seven seas an' done black things! An' all I had ta do was ask.' " John took a breath so deep it puffed out his cheeks when he let it out.

"What did you say?" Sarah demanded, although he had already told her the story a half-dozen times.

"That it was the best present anyone ever gave me. It was, too," he fiercely added. "Klaus said he was charting a new course, then told me again to 'git.' "

Sarah sighed. "I wish I could have been there."

John shook his head. "I'm glad you weren't. Klaus was so sick that when I first saw him, I didn't recognize him. It's funny, but I don't remember him that way now. I just remember how happy and excited he looked that he'd found Jesus." He felt Sarah's hand fall away from his arm and glanced at her. "Sarah, are you listening? You wanted me to tell you the story."

She gave a little cry and sprang forward. John whipped back around and stared after her. "Oh, no!" He thundered after his sister, alarm filling him.

Mother lay on the ground, white and still as a dead person.

Father snatched her up in his arms and raced toward their hut. "John, fetch Dr. Fuller," he ordered. "Tell him she collapsed for no apparent reason. Sarah, run ahead and spread the mattress."

John took one look at his father's ashen face. "Shouldn't you take her to the common house?"

"Nay. Home is closer. Go, lad, and don't stop to argue!"

John turned and ran as if pursued by a thousand howling wolves. Dread kept time to his flying steps. Would Mother be taken next? It hardly seemed fair, when she had worked so hard to care for others, with no thought of risk to herself. "Please, God, spare her. Not just for our sake, but for the sake of others who need her so much." John's prayer came out in little jerks.

Minutes felt like a lifetime before Dr. Fuller reached the Smythes. John had delivered his message and flown home without waiting for the physician. The kindly, overworked doctor bustled in. "Eh, what's all this? Is my best helper giving out on me?" He quickly examined Mother, who didn't even move.

John held his breath, waiting. Sarah stood more still than a mouse that suspects a cat may be nearby. Father sat on the homemade bench, head bowed. John knew he was praying.

Dr. Fuller finished his examination, rose from beside the straw mattress, and smiled. It sent hope to the faces of the waiting family.

"Now, now, nothing to worry about." His face crinkled into laugh wrinkles. "She's just plain worn out. Bodies keep going and going when we push them. How well I know!" He yawned mightily.

John felt his nerves would snap. A look at Sarah showed she felt the same.

"Your wife has no fever," Dr. Fuller said to Father. "She has no signs that foretell illness. I'd say what she needs is a good night's sleep. Don't wake her, even for food. Her body needs rest." He yawned again. "In fact, that's what I'm going to do: rest. My patients have either died or are mending."

He shook hands with Father and John, then tugged on a braid that showed beneath Sarah's cap. "It's your turn to play nurse, Mistress Smythe. See that you do a good job."

"I will," Sarah promised.

Dr. Fuller went out, leaving the others to follow his orders.

The rest of the day, Mother lay without moving. Once when Father and Sarah weren't looking, John bent low to make sure she still breathed. He felt her slow, steady breath against his cheek and sighed in relief. But when evening came and the Sabbath ended, Mother still slept.

"Should we ask Dr. Fuller to come again?" Sarah anxiously asked Father. John silently echoed the question.

"I hate to disturb him when he is so tired." Father knelt

and touched Mother's forehead. "Her skin is cool and dry. She has no sign of fever. We will let her rest."

"Shall I stay up with her?" Sarah volunteered.

"Should Dr. Fuller be wrong, although I have no reason to believe this is the case, you will be needed more on the morrow. Go to bed, child. I will watch."

All through the long night hours, Mother slept. Neither did she waken when morning came. Thoroughly alarmed, John coaxed Father into letting him bring the doctor. After Dr. Fuller examined Mother, he assured them again that she would be fine. "I expect her to wake before night," he told them. "If she should not, then is time enough to be concerned."

Shortly after he left, a sound from the mattress brought all three watchers to Mother's side. She opened her eyes, yawned, stretched, and looked around. "Mercy, what am I doing here at this time of day?"

Memory returned. "My goodness, I fell asleep walking home, didn't I? I never heard of such a thing." She glanced around the hut. "I hope you ate without me." A frown wrinkled her forehead. "I smell something cooking. Surely you are not breaking the Sabbath by cooking food!"

"It's no longer the Sabbath," John shouted. A broad grin spread over his face. Matching smiles covered Sarah's and Father's faces.

Father reached down a hand to help Mother get up. "It's Monday and time for dinner. You have slept ever since the meeting yesterday."

"Dr. Fuller said we weren't to disturb you unless you didn't wake before dark," Sarah explained. She clasped her arms around her mother's waist. "I'm glad you're awake. It frightened me when you stayed asleep for so long."

Mother began to laugh. She laughed so hard the others joined in. "A grown woman, sleeping all the hours on the clock twice around! I do feel rested, though." She looked ashamed. "I hope no one needed me."

Father shook his head. "Not even Dr. Fuller. He says the worst is over and his patients are mending." The laughter in his eyes died. "Almost every family but ours lost at least one person."

A lump came to John's throat. "We lost Klaus."

"Indeed we did, although we haven't actually lost him. We've just parted for a time." Father looked with joy at Mother. "Let us give thanks for your mother's recovery."

Signs of spring began to appear at Plymouth Colony like a long-awaited guest. They brought a wave of relief and hope. Surely things would be better now that the harsh winter was slowly retreating. The little band of remaining settlers prayed for good weather, asking the Lord to bless the land. Yet many of those who survived were still weak. How could the few strong ones left in the settlement take on extra duties and provide for everyone?

There was also the ever-present fear of Indian attack, although except for the scouting party skirmish and a few sightings, there had been no trouble.

One day in mid-March, John burst into the Smythe home as if chased by a whole tribe of unfriendly Indians. Eyes wide with excitement, he cried, "Mother. Father. Sarah, come quick. Just come see!"

John frightened Sarah so badly, she dropped her knitting. "Father and Mother are at the common house. John Smythe, is this another of your tricks? Just when you've been good for such a long time?"

"It's not a trick," he indignantly told her. "Are you coming, or aren't you? If you don't, you'll miss all the excitement." He placed his hands on his hips and glared at Sarah. "C'mon, will you? Father and Mother will have heard the news. They'll be there before I get back with you." He hurried out the door and started up the lane.

Sarah quickly took care of her knitting and ran after him toward a cluster of people on the road a little way ahead. They headed straight for Father and Mother, who stood at one side of a small gaping crowd.

"What is it?" Sarah stood on tiptoe, trying to see.

"Him!" John stepped out of her way and pointed to a tall, black-haired Indian halfway across the clearing between the settlement and the woods. The Indian carried bow and arrows and steadily walked toward the nearest group of men.

"Is he going to scalp us?" Sarah squeaked.

The men reached for their muskets. The Indian never faltered. He was close enough now so the settlers could get a good look. Sarah knew her eyes grew large as cart wheels. She felt herself blush and quickly looked away. So did the other girls and women. The unexpected visitor wore no clothes. Just a little war paint and a leather apron that hung down from his belly! Who was this bold Indian who marched into the colony instead of skulking in the woods?

He reached the men. "Welcome." The word sounded strange on the lips of the nearly naked man. "Samoset."

"Did you hear that?" John whispered. He speaks *English!*"

"What is a samoset?" Sarah whispered back.

John choked. "Not a samoset. Samoset. That must be his name."

Sarah risked another look, making sure she kept her gaze on the stranger's face. "Why did he come here, and what does he want?" she wondered.

"That's what we need to find out," Father said. Some of the same boyish excitement in John's face brought color to his own. "Son, come with me so we can hear better."

Sarah tried to hide her disappointment as Father and John left her and Mother and walked straight toward Samoset. If only she could hear the Indian's words herself!

CHAPTER 13

Hair-raising Stories

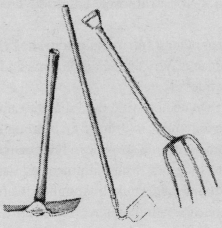

The first thing Samoset did was ask for something to drink. The settlers quickly took on their role of hosts, and once his thirst was satisfied, Samoset told his story.

Samoset explained he wasn't from the area but came from Monhegan, an island off the coast farther north. He said in broken English that he had learned the white man's language from English fishermen there. To prove he told the truth, Samoset mentioned the names of many captains who fished there.

He'd come to Cape Cod the year before and remained eight months. He added he could reach his home with one day of good sea breeze, but it took five days to go by land.

Fascinated by the visitor, the Pilgrims brought out a long, red, horseman's coat. Samoset wrapped himself in it, grunted, and talked on. The settlers brought food: butter, cheese, a slice of duck, and some kind of pudding. He ate and ate and talked and talked! Sarah and Mother and the other women had long since gone, but Father and John stayed and listened. It appeared Samoset had no intention of leaving.

"What will we do with him?" John whispered. Even in the red coat that covered his nakedness, Samoset was a frightening figure.

Others wondered the same thing. The Pilgrims decided to take Samoset to the *Mayflower* but ran into trouble. A head wind and low water made it impossible to get the shallop across the flats to the ship. Stephen Hopkins at last agreed to keep Samoset overnight and guard him without seeming to do so.

"I wish *we* could have quartered Samoset," John grumbled to Sarah later. "Think of all the stories he could tell us! Now we'll have to hear them from the Hopkins family."

Sarah's mouth turned down. "At least you got to hear him

this afternoon, which is more than I could do. Anyway, I'm glad we don't have to keep him. He might tell us stories of how the Indians scalp people."

John grinned mischievously. "I guess you could say they would be hair-raising tales, couldn't you?"

Sarah's green eyes flashed. Her freckled nose went into the air. "Humph! You won't think it's so funny if we wake up murdered in our beds."

"If we're murdered in our beds, we won't wake up," John answered. When his sister's face turned red, he quickly added, "Don't be mad, Sarah. I was just joking. Besides, if Samoset were unfriendly, he would never have come right into the settlement. He'd have brought a band of warriors."

Sarah finally agreed, and John said no more about hair-raising tales.

The next day Samoset left, the proud possessor of a ring, knife, and bracelet. He promised to come back with some of the Wampanoag Indians who would bring beaver furs for trade. The next time Samoset came, he arrived on a Sunday with five tall Indians wearing deerskin clothes.

"It's too bad they came today," Sarah said. "We can't trade on Sunday."

"It *is* awkward," Father admitted. "Our leaders will just have to explain we don't trade on Sunday."

John ran up to his family, bursting with news. "Wait til you hear what's happened," he shouted. "You'd never guess, not in a million years!" He didn't give them even a minute to answer but said, "The tools. *The Indians brought back the tools they stole from us.*"

Mother clapped her hands, and Sarah cried, "Then they must be honest." She stopped and wrinkled up her face. "If they are honest, why did they take our tools in the first place?"

The same funny feeling John had known weeks earlier came back. He lowered his voice so no one else could hear. "What's the difference between our taking their corn and them stealing our tools?"

"Your mother and I have never felt comfortable about that," Father quietly said. "Even though our leaders have vowed to repay the Indians when the crops are harvested."

Samoset soon brought someone else to the settlement, an Indian named Tisquantum, or Squanto. Squanto's life had been hard. John listened in wonder as Squanto told his story. Years ago, a captain named Weymouth had explored the northern New England coast. He took Squanto back to England with him. There the Indian learned to speak the white man's language.

Nine years later, Squanto sailed back across the Atlantic as interpreter to Captain John Smith. A man named John Hunt commanded one of the ships. Hunt persuaded twenty Indians, including Squanto, to board his ship.

John burned with anger when he learned what happened next. Hunt kidnaped the Indians, took them to Spain, and sold them for twenty pounds each! Pride filled Squanto's face and he drew himself up with great dignity. "No Patuxet shall be slave to a white man. I escaped to England, lived with a merchant, then sailed to Newfoundland as a guide and interpreter." Two years ago, Squanto had returned to his home of Patuxet.

A sad look came into the Indian's dark eyes. He placed one hand over his heart. "Plague had killed all but a few of my tribe. Those who yet lived had joined the Wampanoag and their mighty warrior chief, Massasoit. I found them and also stayed with the Wampanoag."

Governor Carver asked, "Squanto, will you not stay and help us? You have lost most of your people. So have we. Sickness and starvation have taken more than half our number since we came a few months ago. Our food is almost gone. We want no trouble with your people."

Squanto turned his glittering gaze on the governor and crossed his arms over his chest. His voice rolled out like a judgment. "Chief Massasoit and the Wampanoag are very angry. The white men stole their corn."

"We did that, and it was wrong," Governor Carver admitted. "Our people were starving and needed food. We will replace the corn when we harvest our fields."

Squanto grunted. John had the feeling he admired Governor Carver for being so honest. John remembered his father telling him that Indians respected courage, and it surely took courage to confess to stealing the corn and to admit it wasn't right.

"I will stay. First, I will talk with Chief Massasoit. If he will come, I will bring him to you so our tribes might have peace."

He turned and marched away.

Samoset and Squanto had been bold but friendly. Chief Massasoit and his twenty scantily clad warriors, however, strode into New Plymouth as if it belonged to them! Massasoit appeared to be a few years older than Squanto and stood as tall and straight as one of the arrows he carried. Chief Massasoit kept his kingly air all through the hearty meal and gifts brought to him by the Pilgrims. At last the time came to talk about peace. Squanto interpreted.

After a brief battle with his conscience, John had tucked himself into a good place so he could see and hear without being noticed. Missing the meeting between Chief Massasoit and the governor was unthinkable, but John knew better than to ask Myles Standish for permission to be present. Every time the captain looked at him, his glare shouted he hadn't forgotten a certain John Smythe's disobedience.

John tried to memorize every detail so he could faithfully pass them on to Sarah. Massasoit, king of the Indians, was indeed a fearsome sight. He sat on cushions. Sweat and grease covered his head and red-painted face. White bone beads, a knife on a string, and a tobacco pouch hung from his neck. His warriors also had painted faces: red, white, black, yellow. John was glad that they had come on friendly terms. He wouldn't want to meet them in the woods otherwise!

Governor Carver and Massasoit talked for a long time. At last, they made a treaty. John listened carefully to Squanto's explanation of the agreement. Neither Massasoit nor any of his people would hurt the Pilgrims. If any of his people did hurt a Pilgrim, Chief Massasoit would send the guilty person to the Pilgrims for punishment. If any of the Pilgrims harmed an Indian, the Pilgrims would turn the person over to Chief Massasoit.

If any tools were taken, the chief would see they were restored. If anyone made war unjustly against either the Pilgrims or the Indians, the other group would provide protection.

Chief Massasoit also promised to send word of the treaty to his neighboring tribes, so they would follow it as well. The Indians would leave behind their bows and arrows when they visited the Pilgrims. The settlers would do the same with their muskets. Through this treaty, King James would recognize and honor Massasoit as his ally and friend.

After the meeting, Governor Carver escorted Massasoit to the brook with great ceremony and bid him a courteous good-bye. When John reported it to Sarah, he said, "They actually put their arms around each other and hugged!"

"Really?" Her eyes opened wide.

John nodded. "Yes." He threw his cap into the spring air. "At last, things are better, Sarah. Squanto and Samoset have agreed to help us plant corn and spend the summer nearby."

Soon the Pilgrims found it hard to remember when Squanto had not been among them. He knew so much! He showed them how to raise the finest corn, beans, and pumpkins by planting dead herring with the seeds. He taught them the best places to fish and how to get eels. Sarah turned up her nose at those!

Everyone who could worked hard. Sarah, John, and Mother, along with the other women and children, spent long hours in the fields. Father and the rest of the men cleared and tilled land. What little time they had at home was gobbled up by other tasks. Furniture making, candle making, spinning, weaving, sewing, shoemaking, and a hundred other duties cried out to be done.

Father and John stole what time they could to fish. Although they both enjoyed fishing, they needed to catch lots of fish to help make a living. Dried fish shipped to markets in Europe could be traded for cloth and other needed supplies.

Other men caught whales so they could send whale oil to Europe. John Alden continued his cooper business. A blacksmith also served as a dentist.

In early April, a silent group of settlers stood on shore watching the *Mayflower* set sail for England. Not one Pilgrim had accepted Captain Jones's offer to take anyone who wanted to sail back with him. Sarah winked back a tear. Would she ever see Holland again? Or the Dutch friends she and John had skated and played with? She sighed. "Father, will we ever go ho—back?"

Father watched a strong breeze fill the sails of the *Mayflower* and move her out of the harbor toward the wide Atlantic. "Nay, child. This is our home now." He placed one arm around her shoulders, his other around Mother, and smiled at John. "God is good. He has brought us safely through the winter. We are at peace with Chief Massasoit and his tribes. We have much to be thankful for."

"We mustn't forget Squanto," Mother said. "Surely God sent him to us, that we might learn to live in this new land."

John said nothing. He wouldn't go back to Holland if he could. Yet seeing the *Mayflower* move toward the horizon where it would dip out of sight brought back memories. The crossing. The poor food and lack of good water. The storms that threatened to tear the ship apart at the seams. Most of all, Klaus.

John hadn't been back on the *Mayflower* since his friend died. Would Captain Jones and the small crew who must battle their way across the heaving seas miss the rough seaman? John turned away to hide his feelings. Better to do as Father said and be glad that life was not as hard as it had been during the winter.

But the peace of New Plymouth exploded a few days later. John and Sarah were working together in the fields near Governor John Carver. Suddenly he clutched his head and groaned. He staggered toward his home.

John and Sarah continued working, but they watched anxiously as Dr. Fuller hurried to Governor Carver's home. It seemed like the doctor stayed with the governor for an eternity. When he finally left the governor's home, Dr. Fuller's face was grim.

Sarah and John looked at each other. Was Governor Carver only the first? Were any in the colony strong enough to survive a second round of sickness?

CHAPTER 14

Danger for Squanto!

The Smythe family and all the other Pilgrims prayed for Governor Carver to get well, but just a few days after he fell ill, he died. The whole colony mourned.

"Pray for me, Sarah," John confided as he solemnly prepared his musket. All the men and boys who had muskets were going to fire off volleys of shot in honor of Governor

Carver. "I don't want to shoot at the wrong time or do something stupid," he admitted to his younger sister.

Sarah gave his arm an encouraging squeeze. "I know you'll do fine," she said, "but I'll pray for you anyway."

Somberly, the Smythe family joined their neighbors outside in the warm spring air. When the time came for the muskets to be fired, John fell into line and paid careful attention to the orders that were given. His hands were sweaty from nervousness, so he quickly wiped them on his pants so that his finger wouldn't slip off the trigger. Boom! Boom! The sounds of the shots echoed across the settlement.

John sighed in relief and threw a grateful look at Sarah. He'd managed to stay out of trouble ever since that terrible night in the woods, and he was grateful nothing he'd done during this important event had drawn attention to himself.

Shortly after Governor Carver was buried, the men of New Plymouth voted for a new governor. John knew better than to try to sneak into that meeting, but he and Sarah were glad to learn from Father that William Bradford would be their next governor.

Now that spring had arrived, Sunday meetings were more pleasant. No longer did they have to bundle up in all the clothing they possessed to keep from freezing in the unheated meetinghouse.

"I wish the tithingman would go away," John complained to Sarah one Sunday. He rubbed his head. The tithingman's rod had feathers on one end to tickle those who nodded, a knob on the other to whack those who fell asleep. He walked up and down checking on people and had given John a smart whack! Sarah took care to sit up straight on the hard wooden pew and concentrate on the elder in the high pulpit. Yet even she found it hard to pay attention. Sometimes the sermons lasted five hours!

"At least I didn't have my neck and heels tied together and get left without food for a whole day," John soberly said. "That's what the governor ordered when John Billington refused to take his turn standing guard at night. He would have carried it out, too. It's a good thing Mr. Billington said he was sorry and would keep watch for strange Indians and fire, like the rest of the men."

"Let's talk about happier things," Sarah pleaded. She didn't like to think of people breaking the rules and being punished. "Did you know Edward Winslow and Susanna White are getting married?"

"Yes. I heard they have both been lonely since Mistress Winslow and William White died." John squinted his eyes against the bright sun. "Sarah, if Mother or Father died, do you think the other one would get married again?"

Sarah thought for a moment. "Perhaps. They'd want us to still have a mother and father."

John shrugged. "I'm not sure I like the idea. Can you imagine anyone ever taking Mother and Father's place?"

"I don't want to think about it," Sarah said. "I'm so tired of death and dying. I hope all of us who are left live to be as old as the mountains!"

"Maybe we will." He flexed his right arm, proud of the muscle that popped up. "Now that Squanto has taught us how to fish and plant, we shan't go hungry." He laughed. "Do you want to hear something funny?"

"Of course."

"I asked Squanto how he knew the very best time to plant maize and the seed we brought with us," John explained.

"What did he say?" Sarah promptly forgot to be sad. Over time, she had learned not to be afraid of Squanto.

"He told me the time of planting must always be 'when the leaves of the white oak are as large as a mouse's ear.' "

Sarah chuckled. "A big mouse's ear, or a little mouse's ear?"

"Can you imagine Squanto's face if I asked him that?" John demanded. He crossed his arms over his chest, planted his feet apart, and deepened his voice. "White boys ask too many questions."

"You sound just like him!"

"I know." John went back to his normal voice. "I like Squanto. He has been so good to us. He. . .he's almost as good a storyteller as Klaus." A shadow crossed his face and he quickly added, "We have to go back to hoeing. Now that the maize is growing so well, it's hoe, hoe, hoe." He started off.

"I think it's pretty, all green and in rows." Sarah looked over the large cleared space. "Father said we prepared nine-ty-six thousand hillocks and trapped and carried forty tons of dead fish to make the crops grow!" She looked at her small hands. Calluses from hard work marred the pink palms. Her short nails required constant scrubbing to keep clean. "I guess it will be worth it when the harvest comes."

Because friendly relations had been established with the Indians, a new problem arose. Throughout the spring and into the summer, groups of visitors came regularly, always expecting food. In desperation, two ambassadors were chosen to go see Massasoit and ask him to call a halt to the frequent visits. The Pilgrims simply didn't have food to spare. Edward Winslow and John Hopkins served as ambassadors, with Squanto as guide and interpreter. John wanted to go with them and longingly watched the three set out.

To the travelers' dismay, Massasoit had very little food, for he had only recently arrived at his home. What little the visitors were given and a few bits of fish on the way home barely provided strength enough for them to again reach New Plymouth.

John eagerly listened when Edward Winslow told the story. "We had nothing to eat the first day. The next morning was used in sports and shooting. About one o'clock Massasoit brought two boiled fishes that were supposed to feed forty people!" He groaned and patted his stomach. "If we had not had a partridge, I fear we should have starved. Swarms of mosquitoes meant we could not stay outdoors. Being crammed together with Massasoit, his wife, and two other chiefs on bare planks on the floor, to say nothing of the fleas and lice, made sleep impossible. We knew Massasoit felt ashamed he could offer us nothing better. We told him we wished to keep the Sabbath at home and departed on Friday before the sun rose."

John hugged his knees, secretly glad he hadn't gone. Adventuring was fine. Being hungry and eaten alive by insects was not!

Another Indian came to live with the settlers. Hobomok was a member of Massasoit's council. Captain Standish made a special point of winning his friendship, but Squanto loyally served Governor Bradford.

One day Hobomok and Squanto went to Nemasket, an Indian camp about fifteen miles to the west. There they hoped to arrange for trade between the colonists and the Indians.

A few days later, Hobomok raced into the settlement. "Squanto has been murdered!" he gasped. His long hair hung in strings. Sweat beaded his frightened face.

"The Nemasket chief Corbitant hates the English. He started a quarrel with us. He tried to stab me, but I escaped. It is said Corbitant has also helped the mighty Narragansetts take Massasoit." His chest rose and fell from his hard run.

Governor Bradford immediately said, "I need volunteers to go with Captain Standish. We cannot allow this thing to go unpunished. Doing so would encourage more such incidents. No Indians would ever again dare be friendly with us. Corbitant and others like him will first kill them, then massacre the colonists. Men, who will go?"

John Smythe bit his lip to keep from shouting, "I will!" Such childish behavior would immediately bar him from the expedition. Instead, he hurried to his father, who had already stepped forward. "Take me with you," he said. "Please?"

Father hesitated. He gave John a measuring look, then turned to Captain Standish. "The lad's wiry body and fleetness of foot might be of use."

Standish looked at John with cold eyes. "That it might. Has he learned to obey orders and will you be responsible for him?"

John squirmed and felt guilty when Father said in a clear, ringing voice, "He has and I will." How could Father have that much faith in him? John resolved to try even harder to avoid trouble.

"See that he stays out of the way," Standish ordered. "If I need him, I'll say so. Otherwise, he's to keep back." A somber look came to his face. He wheeled toward John. "I do not expect that those of us who bear arms and attack shall all be killed. If we are, you must run as you have never run before and carry the news to Governor Bradford. Should the Indians kill us, they will be wild with triumph, perhaps crazy enough to launch an attack on the colony."

"Yes, sir." Although John's throat dried with fear at Standish's words, he kept his gaze level and saluted. His heart thudded against his ribs and he fell into line. It had been months since his last expedition, and then it had been to explore and discover food. Going into the night for the purpose of finding and destroying Indians was far different.

Would any of the men, even Father, come back alive? Yet the murder of Squanto could not be ignored. *Please, God,* he silently prayed. *Keep us safe.* No other words would come. Even though Corbitant and his followers were the enemy, John could not pray for their deaths.

With Hobomok as guide, the party set out for Corbitant's camp. John knew he would never forget that August night. Every rustle of brush rang in his ears. The muffled steps of his companions sounded like thunder claps. Surely any listening Indian could hear the hard beating of his heart.

At last they reached their destination. The rescue party fired their muskets into the air. A wave of terror filled the Indian village. Men, women, and children were ordered not to stir, and Captain Standish marched into Corbitant's hut.

"Corbitant isn't here," Captain Standish called minutes later.

The next instant, some braves made a dash for the woods, straight toward the spot where Father had pushed John down behind a log and ordered him to stay! John flattened himself on the ground and shoved his face in his arms. Shots rang out, followed by cries. John burrowed deeper behind the log. Then a shout brought him to his feet.

"Come, John. The danger is past." Father reached for John's hand and then pointed to a tall figure.

"Why, it's Squanto," the boy gasped. "I thought he was dead!"

"Neither dead nor injured," Father explained. "The people

here know nothing of Corbitant's wicked doings. See, they are bringing food."

"But the shots!" John protested. "Men cried out."

"Some of the Indians were frightened by us and were afraid we had come to harm them. They tried to run away, and our men, thinking those who were fleeing were working with Corbitant, started shooting. Three of the Indians were injured by musket fire, but they will be fine," Father assured him. "Thank God there was no more bloodshed than this. The rumor about Massasoit appears to be just that—a rumor. Captain Standish says we shall take the wounded braves back to the settlement and dress their wounds. We will keep and care for them until they are able to travel back to their own people. This will bring good will between us and the Indians."

John suddenly felt weak in the knees. At last he had been in an actual raid. But Indian braves had been injured in the attack. He decided that fighting the Indians was not as exciting as he had thought. It was terrible!

"Were you frightened?" Sarah asked when he told her about it later.

"Yes, I was," he confessed.

She didn't answer for a time. Finally she asked him quietly, "Do you still want to go adventuring?"

"Yes, but not on Indian raids. I'd rather be a fisherman than an Indian fighter. Does that make you happy?"

Her green eyes shone. "More than I can say."

Her honesty made John want to be just as honest with her.

"All the time I was lying behind that log, I thought how awful it would be to have to run back with news of a massacre! Or how you'd feel if Father or I got killed. I still like adventuring—hunting animals for food and discovering new things. I *don't* like hunting people. Perhaps we have to in order to protect our settlement, but if we could just have peace, I'd be happy."

"So would I." Sarah slipped her hand in his, then ran off to help her mother, leaving John to wonder what would happen next in Plymouth Colony.

Thanksgiving and Fortune

For the next month, many of the Indian chiefs praised the settlers for the way they had handled the incident. Some sent messengers from many miles away to offer their tribes' friendship. Others claimed themselves to be loyal subjects of King James. To everyone's surprise, even Corbitant offered peace through King Massasoit.

Autumn brought more work: John and Sarah spent hours with their neighbors preserving and drying as much food as possible from their small harvest. They had already dried berries and fruit that had ripened earlier in the year. They did not intend to go hungry this winter! The men explored more of the country around them, made treaties with other tribes, and traded trinkets to the Indians for beaver skins.

Then great news came. John burst into the Smythe home and shouted, "Mother. Sarah. Governor Bradford has declared a celebration, and it is to last three whole days!"

"When?" Sarah demanded. "Why? Who is it for?"

"Soon," John told her. "It's a time for giving thanks that God has brought us through our first hard months in the New World. Everyone in New Plymouth will join together *and*. . ." John hesitated to make his news more impressive. "Massasoit and his tribe are to be our honored guests!"

A broad grin spread over his face, making him look more like the mischievous boy who had boarded the *Mayflower* than the young man he had become. "Squanto says we may have ninety Indians here for the feast."

"Ninety? Mercy on us," Mother gasped. "Think how much time it will take to prepare enough food for one meal, let alone three days of celebration!"

"Governor Bradford says everyone in the colony must help." John was thoroughly enjoying himself. "The Indians have promised to bring deer and wild turkeys. Four of the men have been sent to kill wild ducks and geese. Father and I will join others in fishing, plus gathering shellfish and eels."

"I suppose the girls and women will have to cook all this."

Sarah made a horrible face. "Well, someone else can take care of the eels, slimy old things."

"You don't have to do all the cooking," John promised. "Governor Bradford says the younger children are to turn the great spits over the open fires where the meat roasts. They also will gather nuts and watercress."

"We will have to make great kettles of corn and beans," Mother planned. "Oh, my. Think of the baking. We will need journey cake and cornmeal bread and—"

"Be sure to make enough food," John interrupted. "Indians are always hungry." He grinned. "Me, too." His mouth watered. "I hope they don't eat up all the good things before I get a chance at them."

"Remember, son, they are our guests and will naturally be served first," Mother said firmly, but her eyes sparkled with fun. "However, I can't imagine there not being enough food for all."

"There isn't room in the common house or any of the other houses," Sarah pointed out. "How can we feed so many people?"

"The men will lay planks on sawhorses," John said. "We'll eat outside."

Sarah peered out the open door at the warm, mid-October sunshine. "God has already decorated for our feast, hasn't He?" She smiled.

"Indeed he has," Mother agreed. "I have never seen a more beautiful sight than the colored leaves against the dark green forest. There were times when I wondered if we would all be here to see them together."

"Why, Mother! You never told us you were afraid," Sarah said in wonder.

Mother wiped her eyes with one corner of her apron. "Every time I cared for the sick, it was as though I cared for one of you or Father."

John and Sarah looked at each other. How hard it had been for Mother, who had bravely kept her fears to herself for the sake of her family. Sarah put her arm around her mother's waist and whispered, "It's all over now."

"Yes, child." Mother's beautiful smile bloomed like a flower after rain. "Now is a time for giving thanks to our heavenly Father. Come. There is much to be done."

"Mother spoke well," John told Sarah days later when the feast began. "I never, ever saw so much food, not even in Holland."

"That's 'cause we didn't have almost a hundred hungry Indians coming for dinner!" Sarah giggled. She nodded toward the brown-skinned people who had swarmed into the settlement. "Does Massasoit ever laugh? I'm not afraid of Squanto now, but Chief Massasoit makes me feel a little strange when he comes. He's so serious—perhaps because he is the king."

"He is serious, but look at his people. They're really having a good time."

Sarah couldn't help staring. The tribes chattered away in

their own language. They laughed and poked one another in the ribs, evidently sharing private jokes. And how they ate!

"Are you sure there will be any food left for us?" John questioned. "You'd think the Indians hadn't eaten for months."

Sarah rolled her eyes. "If you had helped prepare as much food as Mother and I did, you wouldn't ask such a question. If I never see a dish of succotash again it will be all right with me."

John liked the games and contests almost as much as the food. He won some of the races and enjoyed playing stool ball, a game in which a leather ball stuffed with feathers was driven from stool to stool.

Sarah liked the parade best. One man blew a trumpet. Another beat a drum. Men marched and fired their guns. But Sarah wasn't sure what she thought of the Indian dancing. Their dances were beautiful to watch, but the chants they danced to made chills race up and down her spine.

At last the three-day celebration ended. The great mounds of food were no more. Thanks and praise to God for His goodness still echoed throughout New Plymouth. John patted his full stomach and watched the Indians prepare to leave. "I hope we have another feast next year," he told Sarah.

"It was hard work, but so do I," she said. "I don't know if we will, though." She sighed. "If only all the Indians were our friends we could eat together and have peace. They aren't. The Narragansetts hate us. Remember the snake skin tied to the bundle of arrows they sent? Squanto said it was a challenge that meant they wanted war."

"It didn't frighten Governor Bradford and his counselors," John proudly reminded her. "They refused to back down and returned the snake skin with powder and shot and the message we had done no wrong. The message also said if the Narragansetts would rather have war than peace, they'd find us ready to fight. The arrow came back, but there has been no attack. Don't worry, Sarah. A strong fence surrounds our settlement, and every night a man stands guard. Our men are ready to fight at the first cry of fire or attack." He smiled at his hard-working little sister. "Besides, God has taken care of us so far. Perhaps war will never come."

Sarah already knew all those things, but hearing John repeat them made her feel better.

Early in November, the Pilgrims took stock of their harvest. Their high spirits fell with a thud. The small harvest simply had not produced enough to see them through another winter. Governor Bradford called the people together. "We planned for much larger crops," he soberly said. "Since this did not happen, we must take harsh measures. The ration of meal to each person must be cut in half."

A ripple of protest swept through the assembly. "There is no other way," he told them. "Otherwise, we shall be no better off than we were last year." The people reluctantly agreed they had no choice, but many looked at one another in fear. How could they get by on a half-ration of meal?

A few days later, everyone forgot their troubles for a time.

John brought the news to Mother and Sarah. "A ship is on the horizon," he shouted. "It is coming nearer and will soon anchor in the harbor!"

"Is it the *Mayflower*?" Sarah asked.

John shook his head. "This looks like a much smaller ship. Mother, Sarah, do you think any of our friends from Leiden will be aboard?" His brown eyes sparkled at the idea.

A little worry frown creased Mother's forehead. "Perhaps. I do hope the ship's hold is filled with food supplies. Even by going on half-rations, we barely have enough for those already here."

When the *Fortune* anchored and its passengers came ashore, every person in New Plymouth eagerly awaited them. Fourteen long months had passed since the Pilgrims had left England. Now new, strong people had come to help settle the colony. Supplies from the ship would give strength to continue with the task.

But joy over greeting friends from Leiden soon changed to dismay. Although young and strong, the newcomers were terribly unprepared. They didn't have any food—not even biscuits. They also didn't bring bedding and pots and pans, and most of them had very few clothes. Many of them had sold their coats and cloaks at Plymouth in order to get money for the voyage from England.

"It's not fair," Sarah complained. "They should have brought supplies. Everyone here is tired. Now we have to take these people in and care for them!"

"Didn't God send Samoset, Squanto, and Massasoit to help us?" Father asked. "We will share what we have."

John said, "Those on the *Fortune* felt the same way we did when we first saw Cape Cod. They were afraid we had all been killed in an Indian massacre or died of hunger. The captain said he had just enough food to take the crew on to Virginia. No provisions were sent for the settlers."

Anger grew in him. "John Weston sent a letter bawling us out for not sending cargo back to England on the *Mayflower*. He said the Adventurers are furious and would never have lent us money if they'd known they wouldn't start getting some back soon."

John scowled. "More than half of us died, and all they can think of is their precious money. And John Weston dared to sign himself our very loving friend!"

"I hope Governor Bradford sends a message back telling those people all we have gone through," Sarah indignantly added.

"I am sure he will reply in a manner suited to a godly man," Father quietly told his family. "Just because others are ill-mannered and judge us unfairly does not mean we are to answer in anger."

John hung his head. Would he ever be as patient and good as Father?

By mid-December the *Fortune* was ready to sail back to England. It was loaded with cargo, including many beaver and otter skins that would begin paying off the money that the

Pilgrims owed. Robert Cushman also traveled on the *Fortune,* carrying a contract signed by the Pilgrims. Although the terms were harsh, the colonists had their charter and for the first time were legal owners of New Plymouth.

John and Sarah watched the ship until it disappeared over the horizon. "So much has happened, I wonder what is ahead," Sarah mused.

John gently tugged on one of her dark braids. "Whatever it is, we know God loves and will take care of us." He proudly raised his head. "Governor Bradford says, 'As one small candle may light a thousand, so the light here kindled has shone unto many, yes, in some sense to our whole nation.'"

"As long as the world lasts, people will learn about the Pilgrims and how we came to a land where we could worship God in the way we believed right. More of our people will come, but I'm glad we were the first. I love the New World, don't you, Sarah?"

John anxiously waited for his sister's answer. Did she feel it had been worth it? All the hardship and misery, sickness and death, starvation, and fear of attack?

It has been harder on her than on you, a little voice whispered inside John. *While you chased Indians and got lost in the woods, Sarah could do nothing but worry and pray.* Appreciation for the way she had played a part she never wanted swept through John like a mighty wave.

Sarah waited a long moment. A dozen different expressions crossed her face, mirroring the struggles she had gone through. John saw her glance at the dark, ever-mysterious forest and shiver. She turned toward the sea. Sometimes it danced and sparkled, but it often roared with wind and storm. Last of all, she looked at her brother.

"Well?" John held his breath, hoping with all his heart that in spite of everything, Sarah shared his love for their new home.

She tilted her head back to look up into her tall brother's face. A smile tipped her lips up and a happy laugh rang out in the cold December air. "I love America, too," she said. "I wouldn't want to live anywhere else in the whole wide world." Her words hung in the cold December air, and mischief came into her face. "Race you home!" She took off in a whirl of skirts, happy laughter floating back over her cloaked shoulder.

John watched her go, the courageous sister who had fought fear and won. A year ago he would have let out a yell and caught up with her in a few strides. He'd have passed on long, strong legs, calling out for her to run, not walk. Now he waited, gaze steady on Sarah's flying figure. She had already met and overcome far greater tests than a foot race, but reaching home ahead of her big brother would mean much to her.

"Thank You, God," he whispered, knowing his heavenly Father would understand all the things he couldn't say, just as Mother and Father always did. Making sure Sarah had enough of a head start to win, John grinned and raced after his sister, whooping and hollering all the way.

Good news for readers

There's more!

The Smythe family's exciting story continues in *Dream Seekers*.

John and Sarah have grown up and married, but Phillip and Leah have been added to the Smythe family. Phillip isn't happy. First he had to leave all his friends in Plymouth Colony because his father moved to the Massachusetts Bay Colony. Now he has to put up with his sickly little sister who gets out of all the work but is showered with attention.

Then Phillip and his new friend, Geoffrey, meet a mysterious Indian in the woods near town. Before they can discover whether White Wolf is a threat to the settlers, Geoffrey and his family move. They are following the controversial minister Roger Williams, and they won't be coming back.

Phillips wonders, *Will Leah ever be well? Is White Wolf a friend or an enemy?* And with so much chaos, can Phillip's dreams come true?